By Saria Bryant

ELEMENTAL THRONES
Shadow's Wound
Wild's Scar

TOUCH OF LEATHER
If You Let Me
I'll Give You Everything

UNDERWORLD MAGES
Mage's Marines
Mage's Fugitive

Published by Dreamspinner Press
www.dreamspinnerpress.com

I'll Give You EVERYTHING

SARIA BRYANT

Published by
DREAMSPINNER PRESS

8219 Woodville Hwy #1245
Woodville, FL 32362 USA
www.dreamspinnerpress.com

Trade Paperback ISBN: 9781641088916
Digital ISBN: 9781641088978
Digital eBook published April 2026
v. 1.0

To Axl

Chapter 1

VINCENT CLIMBED out of his car in front of Jasper's place, his fingers itching for the birthday gift he'd forgotten at home, and hesitated, studying the house with a flicker of unease. He'd been back only once since one of Jasper's housemates and a college friend of Vincent's, Matt, dropped his truth bomb about the night his life fell apart ten years ago, and splintered Vincent's worldview.

"You fucking. Left. Me," Matt had snarled. "I let you tie me up, and then you left me there. Did you really think no one would find me like that?"

Vincent didn't remember it that way. He'd been so drunk that most of that night was still full of blank spots where memories should be, but that wasn't much of an excuse. Neither was the fact he'd only finally given in to Matt's pleading because he'd been drunk and grieving. He hadn't spoken to Matt since, not that he blamed Matt for ignoring his texts, but he'd rather fight a heavyweight champion than have another confrontation. Jasper promised Matt wouldn't even be here, but that wasn't a guarantee, considering Matt lived here.

The front door opened, and Jasper hurried out.

Vincent was moving before he thought to, meeting Jasper as he cut through the grass and eyeing the smile that didn't quite reach his eyes. "What's wrong?"

Jasper huffed and stepped into Vincent, fingers twisting his shirt at the small of his back. "Nothing. Just my brother being a dick." He hadn't spoken much about his family in the four months they'd been together, but neither had Vincent.

He slipped his fingers under Jasper's shirt and grounded himself with the feel of warm skin until Jasper stepped away to lead him inside.

Jasper's cousin, Amber, and their housemates were gathered in the living room. Her fiancé, Terrance, sat beside her on the love seat, while Keith and his partner Reiko took the sofa. Matt was nowhere to be seen, but in his place on Reiko's other side was a man Vincent assumed to be

Jasper's brother, though they looked nothing alike. Instead of Jasper's blond hair and blue eyes, his sibling's were both brown.

"Noah, Vincent. Vincent, my brother."

Noah lifted his hand from where his arm was stretched along the back of the couch. "So you're the Daddy Dom."

Vincent raised an eyebrow, not missing the quick movement as Reiko jabbed her arm into Noah's ribs. "No," he replied, smiling at Noah when he repeated the word as a question. He didn't bother to elaborate as he took the only remaining seat in the large chair that matched the sofa set. Jasper sat on its arm, and Vincent hooked him around the waist with a gentle tug, silently inviting him to squeeze in next to him. But Jasper stayed where he was.

Vincent wasn't sure what he'd done to deserve it, but Noah continued his antagonism when he asked, "No present?"

"I'll give it to him at home." Vincent preferred that anyway, all the more so with the hostile atmosphere. He'd been prepared for Matt's blatant hatred, not this surprise animosity from a stranger.

Whatever Noah's response was going to be was interrupted by the doorbell, and Jasper immediately hopped up to answer it. Vincent was left eyeing Noah in silence before he glanced at Amber, who met his gaze with a tight expression and a shrug.

Jasper returned a minute later with a stack of pizza boxes and dropped them on the coffee table.

"Not spaghetti?" Vincent asked. He meant it as teasing, but Jasper made a face at him.

"I'm told that's not a birthday meal."

Vincent eyed the pizza boxes with a frown but didn't comment, the unease he'd felt all day at the thought of being ambushed by Matt slowly warping into an offended outrage. If he'd known this so-called party wasn't what Jasper wanted, he would have made proper plans for tonight. At least he was sure he had all the ingredients for spaghetti at home; keeping them on hand was a matter of course since taking Jasper on as his sub. It'd be easy enough to prepare, but the sauce wouldn't have as long to simmer as he'd like.

Compared to the subpar pizza, even an hour of simmering would be better than this. He ate a single slice and noticed Jasper barely ate half of one himself. By the time everyone had eaten, Vincent had begun to wonder whose idea this was, since there didn't seem to be much effort put into it. Wondered if part of that was delayed fallout from Matt telling the rest of them what really happened the night Vincent got drunk and derailed both their lives, or if Jasper's own family simply had so little regard for him when it came to things that required planning or energy.

Jasper moved to the floor in front of Vincent and wiggled back with his elbows until Vincent obliged and shifted his legs apart enough for him to sit between them. Vincent took the opportunity to bury a hand in blond hair and briefly curled his fingers tight with a slow flex of his wrist. Jasper's fingers dug into Vincent's calf before he turned his head to gnaw on a knee.

"Stop flirting and open your presents," Noah muttered as Terrance got up to retrieve the small pile of wrapped gifts and set them on the coffee table.

Jasper flipped his brother off and reached for the closest one, which was obviously a bottle. Vincent didn't think much of it until Jasper opened it to reveal a cheap bottle of scotch. He wasn't prepared for the sight of liquor or the sudden sour taste on the back of his tongue. Vincent tilted his head and closed his eyes as he focused on breathing.

"Really?" Jasper asked, sounding annoyed, and Vincent latched onto the sound of his voice to help ground himself. "It's not even new. Who knows what you put in this."

Noah snorted. "What, like poison?" he asked dryly. "If you don't want it, give it back. Was just trying to be nice now that you're legal and all."

Jasper shifted in front of him, and he hoped that meant he was giving the bottle back. He didn't dare open his eyes again until he heard the ripping of paper, then risked looking over Jasper's shoulder to see him holding two new games, one for his handheld and one for a console. He kept his eyes on Jasper and his presents to avoid accidentally seeing where the bottle had gone. He'd been sober for ten years, but he'd also curated his life in a way that minimized his exposure to alcohol. Even at the club, his staff knew to inform him the moment anyone checked in a bottle of liquor, and he'd put strict procedures in place both for his own safety and that of his business.

Jasper opened the rest of the presents quickly. A *BDSM for Beginners* guidebook came from Keith, and Reiko gave him a package with fox ears. It was only when Jasper's ears turned red and he shoved the box behind him that Vincent realized it was some kind of sex toy. He reached down to pluck it free, ignoring Jasper's squawk of protest as he studied it. Fox ears and tail, complete with a vibrating plug on the end of the tail.

He slanted a quick glance at Reiko to find her smirking at him and silently cursed ever sharing one of his biggest fetishes with her. He set the package next to the chair as Jasper opened the last gift to find an envelope, only to nearly lose his eardrums when Jasper shouted, "No way! How did you get these? They've been sold out for weeks."

"I called in a favor," Amber replied smugly as Jasper all but threw himself at her for a hug.

"Thank you, thank you, thank you!" He did a happy dance on his way back to Vincent before waving the slender pieces of paper in front of his face.

Vincent took them rather than go cross-eyed and saw they were tickets for a concert for next weekend. That would work well enough with his plan of taking a trip for Jasper's birthday at least.

"You'll take me?" Jasper asked.

Vincent met Jasper's eyes as he handed the tickets back. "Of course."

Jasper beamed at him and tucked the tickets into the envelope, which he stuck in the book.

Vincent held his hand out, and Jasper eyed him in confusion before offering the book over. It was heavy and bound in black leather. When he flipped through the pages, he saw they weren't simply definitions of the more common—and some uncommon—kinks but had details and illustrations too. "Where did you even find this?"

"Specialty shop," Keith replied. "Want the info?"

"Yes, please," he said, closing the book. It'd be a nice touch to add to the club. Jasper rolled his eyes before setting his games on top of the book. Vincent didn't miss the pleading stare that followed, and if not for the fact that seemed to be it for the so-called party, he might not have been willing to leave so soon. There hadn't even been a cake. "Ready to go?"

"Yup!" Jasper replied too brightly, still on his feet. He grabbed his gifts from Vincent, waved, and turned for the door.

Vincent scooped up the package of fox paraphernalia that Jasper was obviously trying to leave behind before saying goodbye. Jasper had a small duffel slung over his shoulder when Vincent caught up to him on the way to the car. Once they were on the road, he glanced over at

Jasper, who was slumped in his seat. "Is there anything else you want to do today?"

"Not really."

"Spaghetti for dinner?" he suggested.

Jasper rolled his head against the headrest to stare at Vincent. "Really?"

"Sure."

He leaned across far enough to rest his head on Vincent's shoulder. "Thanks." He was silent for a few moments before he muttered, "Did you really have to bring the fox ears?"

Vincent drew in a slow breath to make sure his voice was steadily neutral when he asked, "You don't like them?"

Jasper grumbled and bit Vincent's arm, then asked, "Do you?"

He had no reason to hide it, but he was still hesitant to answer. It wasn't only the fox ears that he enjoyed. One of his biggest kinks was role-play, and he'd hoped Jasper would at least be open to that. "Yes," he finally said.

Jasper was silent for a long moment, then pressed his face into Vincent's arm with a groan, which was as endearing as it was confusing.

"What's wrong?"

"Shoulda known you'd want to use them," he grumbled under his breath.

Vincent tried not to get his hopes up. "Do you not want to?" That might not be an outright no, but it wasn't an enthusiastic yes either. But then, new things rarely were with Jasper. It was something he hoped would change as they explored a bit more.

"It's embarrassing," Jasper murmured, so softly Vincent almost missed it over the sound of the car.

Vincent stifled a soft laugh. He was fairly certain Jasper's reactions so far meant he actually enjoyed being embarrassed, but had yet to call him out on it. He didn't press now, either, content to save tormenting him for tonight.

When they reached Vincent's home, he hesitated before shutting the car off. Jasper already had his door open and a foot out before he realized Vincent hadn't moved and turned back in confusion. "What's wrong?"

Vincent cleared his throat against the memory of the sour taste on the back of his tongue. "I don't mind if you drink," he said after a moment, "but I can't have alcohol in my home."

Jasper tilted his head with a slight furrow between his brows, but then he glanced at Vincent's chest and arm, where his scars—the legacy of his past history with alcohol was literally burned into his skin—were hidden under his shirt. With a soft sound of understanding, he said, "Okay."

Vincent wasn't quite expecting such easy agreement. His surprise must have been obvious, because Jasper made a face at him.

"I'm not interested in drinking anyway. Not really. Noah drinks and smokes enough for the both of us. Among other things," he muttered.

Vincent hummed softly and finally climbed out of the car. "He didn't seem to like me much."

Jasper followed after him with a scowl and shut the car door with more force than necessary. "I don't care what he thinks. I'm surprised he even showed up. Not like we've talked much since I was a kid." He stalked into the house and kicked his shoes off by the door. "Gonna put these up," he said on his way up the stairs.

Vincent watched him as he slipped his own shoes off and tossed his keys to the hall table, curious about Jasper's bitter tone and what had caused it, but he obviously wasn't getting answers tonight. With a sigh he headed to the kitchen. If he started the sauce now, it'd at least have a few hours to cook. It didn't take long to put together, and he set the stove to low to let it simmer before going in search of Jasper. He'd expected the brat to hover in the kitchen to see if he was really making spaghetti, but he hadn't heard a peep since Jasper went upstairs. When he stepped into the bedroom he saw why.

Jasper was sprawled facedown on the bed, naked except for the fox ears and tail.

He had a moment to be disappointed at missing the chance to watch Jasper work the plug into himself before he noticed the blindfold already secured around Jasper's eyes. That was something they'd only recently started using, but with amazing results: Jasper tended to be less vocal, less bratty, and somehow even more responsive when he wore one.

Vincent shut the door with a firm click, waited a beat, and flipped the lock for good measure. He stopped at his dresser to pull out a tie, then continued to the bed for a better view. "I seem to have a trapped fox," he murmured. "Whatever shall I do with it?"

He hummed in approval when he spotted the remote for the fox tail, along with lube, on the nightstand and pulled out a condom to set next to them. Then he trailed his fingertips from Jasper's ankle up the inside of his thigh, over his ass, and up his back to his arm. He guided both arms behind Jasper and used the tie to keep them there. Jasper's breathing hitched as Vincent finished securing them.

Vincent let his hand rest on Jasper's bound wrists as he considered, then stayed silent while he tossed the condom, lube, and remote to the bed, rolled Jasper to his side facing away from Vincent, and stretched out behind him. Once they were settled, he studied the remote before turning it to its lowest setting, which caused Jasper to jerk against him with a surprised moan.

Vincent chuckled and pressed his lips to Jasper's neck while lazily exploring his chest. He hooked a hand under Jasper's leg to pull it over top of his own, then snagged the end of the tail to brush the soft fur against Jasper's thighs and erection. When Jasper tried to roll forward and away, Vincent slid his other hand up to rest against Jasper's throat to keep him in place and curled two fingers over his chin to press past his lips.

Jasper whimpered around Vincent's fingers but stopped trying to pull away, wiggling against him instead. It turned to writhing when Vincent turned the plug to a higher setting.

He turned it up another notch, then another, until Jasper let out a pleading whine. He relented and dialed it back down, then turned his attention to Jasper's nipples and neck. The fox items might have been more for Vincent's pleasure than Jasper's, which was a questionable incentive for a gift in his opinion, but that didn't mean he couldn't ensure Jasper thoroughly enjoyed himself.

It didn't take long to reduce Jasper to a panting, moaning mess, especially when Vincent quickly pulled his fingers from his mouth to torment Jasper's nipples. He pinched and twisted and tugged until they were both hard, covered Jasper's neck and shoulder with a dozen marks, then turned the plug to its highest setting. While Jasper thrashed and bucked, Vincent wrapped his fingers around Jasper's cock in a loose hold, refusing to tighten or stroke even when Jasper pushed into his fist, desperate for friction.

Only when Jasper turned his face into the pillow with a long pleading whine did Vincent take pity on him enough to tighten his grip. He even offered a few strokes when Jasper immediately began thrusting.

He waited until he heard the sharp gasping whimpers that meant Jasper was getting close, then pulled his hand away. Jasper groaned in protest, and Vincent smothered a chuckle against his shoulder, running a soothing hand over his hip before reaching for the condom. A few moments to get his pants open and the condom on and lubed up, and another to find the remote and shut the plug off. Then he pulled it free, tossed it aside, and gripped Jasper's thigh to lift his leg before pressing into him.

Jasper tipped his head back as he keened, the soft fox ears brushing against Vincent's face as quiet pleas of *yes* and *more* fell from Jasper's lips.

Vincent pressed his face into Jasper's neck, breathing in his scent and dragging his teeth against the flush-warm skin. He settled into a slow rhythm despite Jasper's begging. No need to rush. Jasper was his for the rest of the week, and while Vincent would still need to go to work at his club, he'd taken the night off to ensure Jasper enjoyed his birthday. Thankfully it fell early enough in the summer break that they had plenty of leeway for their vacation before the next semester started. He hadn't expected tonight to include fox accessories and a blindfold, but the fact Jasper was willing to wear that much offered him some hope that they'd be able to indulge his love of role-play later.

For now he took advantage of his fox, slowly grinding into him while leaving more marks on his neck and shoulder. Jasper tipped his head back and to the side with a whine, seeking a kiss, and Vincent gladly obliged, kissing him with the same unhurried pace as his thrusts.

Any time spent with Jasper was a treat, but kissing him was its own little luxury. He didn't try to control the pace but responded with the same enthusiasm as he did most everything else. When they finally broke apart, Jasper was panting, his lips slick and swollen, soft breathless moans escaping between gasps.

Vincent adjusted their positioning enough to hook Jasper's leg over his own and moved his freed hand to Jasper's hip to keep him steady as he picked up the pace. He caught an earlobe between his teeth and slammed forward with a grunt, hooked his other arm across Jasper's chest as he braced his foot against the mattress, and fucked into him with steady, relentless thrusts.

Jasper bucked against him as best he could, but Vincent ensured he was as restrained as possible. Whenever Jasper neared the edge, Vincent pulled him back with a quick slap to his balls. He did that several times until Jasper was sobbing and begging for release, then finally pressed his lips to Jasper's ear with a soft "Come," while he jerked Jasper off.

Jasper shuddered through his orgasm with a hoarse scream, and Vincent grunted as Jasper tightened around him. A few more thrusts and he found his own release, though he remained buried inside as they caught their breaths, absently stroking his thumb against Jasper's softening cock until he whimpered from the stimulation.

With a quick press of his lips to Jasper's neck, Vincent pulled out and away. It only took a few moments to get Jasper free of the tie, and the ears came off with the removal of the blindfold. Then Vincent disposed of the condom, retrieved a damp cloth from the bathroom, and cleaned Jasper up. He tossed the cloth aside, along with his pants. and settled back into bed, unsurprised when Jasper latched on with all four limbs. He trailed his fingers up Jasper's spine and into his hair, where he curled them into a loose grip that earned a low hum of pleasure.

Jasper passed out as quickly as ever, and Vincent pulled his phone out to set an alarm for an hour before joining him.

BY THE time the alarm went off and Jasper pulled on his boxers and they made it downstairs, the spaghetti sauce had simmered long enough to fill the kitchen with the warm scent of tomatoes, herbs, and garlic.

Jasper filled a pot with water to boil while Vincent set the oven and placed a couple of pieces of cheesy garlic bread on a baking sheet. Once the pot was on a burner, Jasper turned and stepped into Vincent's chest.

Vincent propped a hip against the counter and buried a hand in Jasper's hair. "All right?" he asked, curling his fingers with a light tug when Jasper nodded an affirmative. Vincent tilted his head to press a lingering kiss to Jasper's temple. "Sleepy or subspace?"

"Mm, both?"

Vincent tugged his hair again, enjoying the long, soft moan and the way Jasper melted into him even more. Somehow he managed to get the bread in the oven and the spaghetti into the boiling water without dislodging his new body accessory, but when the food was ready, he had to nudge Jasper into filling a plate.

At the table, he moved his chair close enough to Jasper's that he could rest his left hand on his leg as they ate. "When you're awake enough, I can give you your birthday gift," he said and wasn't disappointed when Jasper straightened with an eager smile, obviously far more alert and present.

"What did you get me?"

"You'll see," Vincent replied dryly, ignoring the pout in favor of eating. When they'd finished, he left Jasper to clean up and retrieved the packets he'd put together from his office. They included several vacation options across the country and two overseas. He set them on the table and waited for Jasper to sit.

"Pick one of these places and we'll go there for two weeks," he said, quickly moving the packs out of reach when Jasper made a sound of excitement and reached for them. "Look through all of them, but the choice is entirely yours. Bring me the one you decide on. I'll be waiting in the playroom."

"Yes, Sir," Jasper said, inching his fingers towards the packets with an innocent smile.

Vincent shook his head and pushed them closer, then mussed Jasper's hair on his way out of the room.

CHAPTER 2

JASPER BOUNCED in his seat as Vincent left, then nearly choked when he picked up the first packet and saw the destination was Paris. He flipped through the pages, but there were no prices anywhere. There were a few places he was sure the price should have been listed, but it was like they'd been erased. He scowled with a soft grumble, but even knowing how expensive a trip overseas was sure to be couldn't dampen his excitement for long.

The Paris packet had several locations that were obviously part of a sightseeing tour. He'd never really given much thought to traveling since it required money and time he doubted he'd ever have, but he wasn't sure Paris was where he'd want to go first. There were other similar packets for New York and California, but it wasn't until he reached one for Tennessee that he found the kind of packet he expected. It was a resort with cabins decked out specifically for BDSM.

He managed to swallow the strangled noise that tried to escape as he flipped through the pages. Most of the pictures were of things in Vincent's own playroom or in the club, so he wasn't sure what the point was in going there when they had all the things they needed here. Then he spotted a packet for a similar resort in the Northwest, tucked away in a wooded area. It was on the outskirts of a small town and had everything from hot springs to zip lining. The pictures of the cabins were almost deceiving, showing a normal living room and kitchen, until he flipped to the playroom. Larger than Vincent's, like the cabin had been built around it rather than it being a room that'd been repurposed.

He set that one aside to give the last packet a cursory glance, but his heart was already set. A few minutes later he picked it back up and took it up to the playroom, where Vincent was waiting for him on the sofa.

Vincent set his phone on the table beside a paddle and held a hand out. "Made your choice already?"

"Yes, Sir." He handed the papers over and sank down beside Vincent. He didn't miss the flicker of surprise as Vincent took the packet.

"You're sure?" he asked, glancing over and resting a hand on the leg Jasper flung across Vincent's lap.

"Yeah? It looks fun. Why?"

Vincent shook his head. "My friend runs this one."

"You mean they're not all run by someone you know?" Jasper asked, grinning when Vincent shot him an unamused glare.

Vincent tossed the papers to the table and picked up the paddle. "Just for that you get an extra few birthday spankings."

"Oh nooo," Jasper replied in mock despair. "Please, anything but that."

He used the paddle to tip Jasper's chin up. "Over my lap, you brat."

Jasper eagerly stretched out over Vincent's thighs and gave a judicious wiggle to get comfortable, but he went still when Vincent slipped a hand between his thighs and adjusted his legs. Heat flooded him when his boxers were pulled down and Vincent proceeded to grope his ass.

"Twenty-one. Plus some extra," Vincent murmured. "You can count them to yourself and tell me when to stop."

"Yes, Sir," he replied, hiding his face in his arms. Even after four months he wasn't used to how easily Vincent touched him, much less how he always seemed to know exactly what Jasper needed. Or how readily he offered anything. It made it *so hard* not to ask for more.

He had no idea where that particular limit was. Vincent was rich enough that Jasper doubted he'd ever get near to reaching *that* limit; he was still traumatized by the amount Vincent had spent on Jasper's damn suit, though he had to admit he looked good in it. And he enjoyed wearing it at the club, knowing it marked him as Vincent's sub.

The first strike of the paddle left him gasping, his attention shattering before refocusing on the already fading sting. Vincent's hand was a warm grounding weight on the center of his back as the paddle landed again. That was two, and warmth was already pooling in his gut despite the incredibly intense sex they had earlier.

Thinking about the fox ears and tail was a mistake. Heat flared in his cheeks and into his ears. He couldn't believe they'd given him sex toys for his birthday, and he really couldn't believe Vincent had been so interested in them. Four months and he knew only a few things Vincent liked for sure: Jasper's bratty attitude, making him taste himself, restraining him at any and every opportunity, and watching Jasper touch himself.

His breath stuttered from the pleasant sting and dull ache from another spank. Four, or was that five?

After a handful of weekends in the club, he knew what few kinks they'd explored were on the tamer side, and Vincent had said at the beginning that his tastes were eccentric. Was he a furry?

He yelped as the paddle struck his thigh hard enough he knew it was already turning red. Fuck. How many was that? He tried to focus on each strike, but the heat building on his ass and thighs was distracting, and every new ache pushed him closer to that comfortable floaty space where nothing mattered except pleasure and Vincent.

He lost count somewhere after fourteen and then completely forgot he needed to count. It felt too good to tell Vincent to stop anyway. He could lie there all night while Vincent turned his entire backside red. He didn't have class or work to worry about. He could handle a sore ass for a day or two.

"Pet," Vincent said after what could have been hours but was likely only minutes. "Did you lose count?"

"Uh-huh."

Vincent snorted and set the paddle on Jasper's lower back before rubbing his palm over the heated flesh of his ass. Jasper whimpered even as he pushed into the touch. "What am I going to do with you?" he asked, sounding amused.

"Fuck me?" Jasper asked hopefully.

"Is that a birthday wish?"

"Absolutely."

Vincent hummed as if considering before lightly smacking Jasper's hip. "I have a better idea."

He couldn't quite swallow a whine—what could possibly be better than having Vincent inside him?—but he obediently got to his feet and watched as Vincent retrieved something from one of the chests. Then he followed to the bedroom and sprawled out in the center of the bed.

"Hands above your head," Vincent ordered as he fished out the lube from the covers, then settled beside Jasper without reaching for any of the restraints hidden beneath the mattress.

Jasper did as told, though he was surprised and worried that Vincent wasn't restraining him like usual. He caught a brief glance at the thin glass plug as Vincent coated it before slowly pressing it into him. It wasn't nearly large enough to do more than tease, but the heat in Vincent's eyes was enough that he didn't complain.

All thoughts of complaining or anything else evaporated when Vincent wrapped a hand around his cock and began stroking, his thumb pressing right beneath the head.

"Deep breaths, pet. And no moving."

Jasper failed to stifle a whimper and squeezed his eyes shut to focus on his breathing. Vincent didn't touch him anywhere else, slowly massaging Jasper's frenulum with his thumb. He wanted to thrust into Vincent's hand or rock his hips to nudge the plug, but he managed to keep still. The pleasure built at an agonizingly slow pace, to the point he was begging for more within minutes.

Vincent's low chuckle sent tingles up his spine, and Jasper couldn't help the way his fingers curled tight in his own hair and tugged. He tipped his head back and groaned as he imagined it was Vincent pulling, relishing the tingles along his scalp.

"Pleeease," he whined, his hips instinctively lifting to push into Vincent's touch before he could stop them.

Vincent *tsk*ed and landed a light slap to his balls. "I said no moving, pet."

Jasper yelped, his eyes flying open at the mix of pleasure and not-quite pain that shot low into his belly. That was a new sensation, and he suddenly wondered why he'd ever marked CBT as a limit if it felt anything like that. He wanted to ask Vincent to do it again, but the words stuck in his throat. Something must have shown on his face anyway, because Vincent chuckled as he dragged his thumb over the head of Jasper's cock.

"Did you enjoy that?" he asked in that low voice that never failed to send shivers of anticipation through Jasper.

"Uh-huh," Jasper breathed, curling his fingers tighter in his hair. "Please, Sir. Do it again," he whispered, trying to ignore the heat creeping into his face. The way Vincent stared at him as his eyes darkened almost made Jasper combust on the spot, but the two quick slaps that followed were even more intense.

Between the occasional jolt of sharp pain-pleasure from his balls, the fingers slowly tormenting the head of his cock, and the earlier spanking, Jasper was riding the edge within minutes. Every time he got close, Vincent's hands would disappear, leaving Jasper hard and aching and desperate enough that his eyes pricked with tears. "Please," he begged, over and over again, nearly sobbing with the frustration until Vincent gave him the friction he needed to finally fall over the edge.

He arched as he came with a sharp cry of relief before dissolving into a breathless laugh. Tremors of pleasure cascaded through his entire body as he sank into the bed. He tried to fight the drowsiness that swamped him, but by the time Vincent had cleaned him up and settled beside him, Jasper was practically unconscious. His last coherent thought was that this had turned into his best birthday ever.

CHAPTER 3

WAKING NEXT to Jasper had quickly become one of Vincent's favorite aspects of having the brat in his home. So when he woke to find Jasper gone and likely making a mess of his kitchen, he was as disappointed as he was satisfied. He stretched, rolled over to find his phone, and squinted against the backlight. Late morning already, so no excuse to let himself fall back asleep.

With a groan he rolled out of bed and made a quick trip to the bathroom. Then he headed downstairs to find Jasper, clad in boxers and a tee, finishing his usual misshapen pancakes and slightly overcooked eggs. One of these days he'd need to take some time to teach Jasper to properly cook them, but for now he settled for wrapping his arms around Jasper's waist and breathing in his scent. The ends of Jasper's hair were still damp from his shower, and his skin still smelled like Vincent's new cedarwood-and-lemon soap. It didn't quite suit Jasper, and he found himself missing the usual citrusy mango scent.

Jasper turned his head to press a quick kiss to Vincent's cheek before scooping half the eggs onto a plate with two pancakes and handing it over. "What's the plan for today?"

Vincent set the plate aside to retrieve the blueberries from the fridge. "Making reservations for vacation, for one. Do you have a preference on when?"

"After the concert? It's next Friday I think," Jasper said, filling his own plate and pouring syrup over his pancakes and eggs.

That was likely too soon to hope for, but he'd call Zach directly to see what they had available. God forbid he try to book online; he'd never hear the end of it. "Double-check after you eat," he said, drizzling some honey over his pancakes before settling at the table.

Breakfast was quick. Jasper was apparently too excited about the prospect of two weeks away from home to do more than inhale his food before racing upstairs to find the concert tickets. Less than a minute later, he was back at the table and shoving them in Vincent's face.

"Next Friday!" Jasper bounced on the balls of his feet, waiting for Vincent to take the tickets before snatching up his abandoned plate and taking it to the sink.

Vincent shook his head, glancing at the date on the tickets before he finished eating. "You want to try for that Saturday?" he asked, getting up to hand his plate over. He found a magnet on the fridge and pinned the tickets to the top corner.

"Yeah, that should give me plenty of time after we get back to get ready for the new semester."

And enough time for Vincent to adjust any living arrangements, though he kept that to himself. He may have offered a second contract, but it was still too early to be considering letting Jasper move in with him, even if Vincent was starting to suspect Jasper's current living situation wasn't the best for him.

He pulled his phone out as he headed down the hall to his office and called Zach.

It rang four times before Zach answered with an exaggerated gasp and a "I didn't know ghosts could use the phone! This is amazing! What's it like on the other side?"

"Ha fucking ha," Vincent replied, barely refraining from rolling his eyes.

"And still the same boring sense of humor. I would have thought the afterlife would cure you of that. I mean, you *are* dead, right? You haven't called in, like, a year, so it must be something extreme."

Vincent winced and stifled a sigh. "I've been busy," he said lamely, settling at his desk and opening his laptop.

"Yes, getting your club up and running. I saw. Congratulations, by the way, even if you didn't invite us to the opening."

Christ. He'd forgotten how thickly Zach liked to lay on the guilt. "I'm sure I invited you when I ordered the benches," he replied. "Same as when you invited me to your resort."

Zach scoffed. "Like fuck Adam would have come out here."

That was true, though listening to Zach tell him how much of a dick Adam was yet again was the last thing he was in the mood for. "I was calling to make a reservation, or should I book it online?"

"What?" Zach audibly perked up. "No way. You found a new sub? Is he cute? Do we get to meet him?"

Vincent nearly shuddered at the thought of Jasper meeting Zach. He didn't need the brat getting new ideas, though he couldn't deny it would likely be good for him to see another sub in his natural habitat rather than at the club. "Maybe. Depends on if you have a cabin available for two weeks, starting next Saturday."

Zach let out a low whistle. "Lemme check. We've started getting booked up pretty far in advance lately." The sound of rapid typing and mouse clicks came through the phone. "So one of the mid-level cabins might be available. Someone reserved it for that weekend, but they haven't paid the deposit yet. Gimme a few minutes."

The complete silence that followed let Vincent know he'd been muted. He put his own phone on Speaker and set it down as he brought up the resort website on his laptop. It didn't take long to find one of the cabins Zach was referring to, and he clicked through the photos available. Two stories, though the top level was a loft with the bedroom and bathroom. A balcony with a nice view of trees and a walking path leading deeper into the woods. Connected den and dining room, large TV, updated kitchen. But the highlight was the playroom.

A bit bigger than Vincent's own, though with a different setup. The obligatory bench, this one in a dark red leather. Handcuffs, crops, and other various impact play items lined one wall, with a couple of chests in the corner. The item that caught his eye, though, was the chair that belonged in a doctor's office. Before he could fantasize too much about how to use it, Zach returned.

"So good news," he said, cheerful grin obvious in his tone. "The cabin is yours, and I've already marked it booked, so you're all set. I assume you'll want supplies brought in?" he asked dryly.

"I'll put the order in if you give me a good day and time for delivery." Vincent wouldn't mind sampling the local restaurants, but more than a few days was too long to go without a proper home-cooked meal, much less two weeks.

"Yeah, sure. Any afternoon that's not the weekend is fine."

"I'll set it for Wednesday, then."

"Sounds good, but you better bring your boy by for dinner."

"I'll suggest it to him."

Zach huffed. "There's a fifteen percent insult fee if you don't. Besides, I know you're gonna want pictures done while you're out here. Ash won't do them without meeting him first. He might make an exception for you, but I'd rather not ask him to."

Vincent winced. "He's gotten worse?" Like Zach, Vincent had met Aston—Ash—in college when he'd transferred overseas after his accident. Unlike Zach, Ash was an extreme introvert and avoided social interactions as much as possible. The two had already been fast friends by the time Vincent met them.

"No, but he has set very firm boundaries over the last year, and that's one of them."

He couldn't exactly say no to that, and it would be a dick move not to visit while he was there. Giving up one evening alone with Jasper wasn't the end of the world. "We'll have dinner."

"Great! What's his favorite food?"

Vincent snorted. "Spaghetti."

"Oh, simple. A boy after my own heart."

He fought back a groan, sure Jasper meeting Zach would end in disaster one way or another, and Vincent had a feeling he'd be the one to suffer from it.

Within a few minutes, he had the room paid for, and they spent another twenty catching up while he put together a grocery order for delivery.

Once that was done, he grabbed his laptop as he went in search of his brat and found he'd made himself at home on the couch with his new console game. Vincent settled in beside him, intending to get the payroll approved and processed for the week, but he found himself distracted by watching Jasper play. He didn't recognize the game, and the gameplay seemed far more challenging than the games he preferred.

After a while Jasper pressed closer and nudged him with an elbow. "Wanna play?"

"I'm good," he replied dryly. He was sure if he took the controller he'd be dead inside of ten minutes. Instead he forcibly turned his attention back to his work. Once the club's payroll was done, he approved the pending time-off requests, set the schedule for the next month, and scheduled an interview for a chef for Tuesday.

Depending on how supplying staff meals went, he'd look into expanding into light dinner options for members who wanted to get to know others better before playing with them. That would be several months in the making, though, so he turned his attention to the other businesses he had a hand in running.

The money his grandfather had given him access to after his mother's death and Vincent's subsequent accident had been spent investing in various stocks, but he'd also needed something more substantial to keep himself grounded amid the chaos of moving back to the States, and he'd found that by getting involved in the local community and businesses. Two were tech start-ups that he'd helped fund shortly after returning from Europe, and he currently held a position on their boards. So long as the owners and CEO remained sensible and their goals stayed aligned, he saw no reason to try to interfere and merely kept up-to-date with any changes they made and the quarterly reports.

Other than the club, his main project was a low-rent apartment complex he maintained in honor of his mother. After choosing love, being disowned, and running away to the States, only for her fiancé to die before Vincent was even born, she was left as a single mother with no work experience in a foreign country. She'd worked three jobs to keep food on their table, and as Vincent got older, he realized how predatory the housing system was.

He could only do so much to help the local community, but having a large apartment complex where those who were on the brink of or were already homeless could get back on their feet was one of the things he chose to do. The ledger might have technically been in the red more often than not, but he kept one of the apartments leased to himself and ensured the monthly rent compensated for any loss on missed or waived payments of the other residents.

The last one was a financial services firm he was a majority shareholder in. He kept a close eye on that one, especially since the reports were a good indicator of changes in the economy.

Once he'd caught up on everything, he set his laptop aside and turned his attention back to Jasper, who was still engrossed in his game. He slipped an arm around his brat and leaned closer to press lingering kisses up Jasper's neck.

"Are you trying to get me killed?" Jasper asked, already breathless.

Vincent hid his smirk against soft blond hair. "Are you that easily distracted?"

Jasper grumbled under his breath, though Vincent caught the word "dick," which he rewarded with a quick bite to Jasper's ear. Then he slipped his hand under Jasper's shirt to caress the warm skin of his side below his somewhat ticklish ribs. The sound of someone dying echoed in the new silence, followed by the splash screen with the options to Retry or Return to Title Menu.

Jasper slowly turned his head to glare at Vincent. "That was your fault."

"I wasn't the one playing."

"Your. Fault. How do you plan to make it up to me, Sir?"

Vincent hummed and leaned in, though he stopped before their lips touched. "There's leftover spaghetti," he murmured, brushing his nose against Jasper's. "And then I'll put you on your knees."

Jasper's eyes darkened as he closed the distance to steal a kiss. "Yes," he groaned, and Vincent restrained his smirk as he took the controller from Jasper's slack grip. He shut off the game and set it on the table, then put Jasper to the task of putting the leftovers to heat in the oven as he headed upstairs.

He had no intention of letting Jasper get off again after indulging him yesterday, but that didn't mean they couldn't enjoy themselves. He gathered the cock cage he'd bought the week before, a simple glass plug, and leather cuffs connected with a short chain. He snagged a small towel from the closet on his way out and deposited everything on the side table by the sofa, then pulled up one of his streaming services to find a movie they'd both enjoy, even if he doubted either of them would be paying much attention.

While they ate, he slipped a foot between Jasper's legs to tease him, enjoying the fidgeting and heated looks. Over four months in and Jasper's responsiveness was still a marvel. Most subs he'd played with in the club, or the few he'd contracted with, he could please easily enough in a scene, but having one so receptive to any attention at all was as thrilling as it was concerning.

Another reason to be torn on whether to offer Jasper the option of moving in with him. Jasper's home life might not seem ideal, but even if they entered into a twenty-four seven lifestyle, Jasper still needed contact with others aside from Vincent. Something to put on the worry-about-later list.

Once they'd eaten and cleaned up, he guided Jasper to the sofa and picked up the cage. Jasper let out a soft moan of anticipation as he glanced from it to the other items. When there was no objection to anything he'd picked out, Vincent peeled Jasper's T-shirt off and trailed his fingers down Jasper's chest and lower. He traced along the hem of Jasper's boxers before pushing them down far enough to drop to the floor. It took a bit of time and adjustment to get the cage on but once it was in place and Jasper realized how constrained he was, he let out a delicious whimper.

Vincent retrieved the cuffs and plug before sitting in the center of the sofa. "On your knees," he ordered, patting the sofa to his right.

Jasper clambered onto the cushions and settled with his knees pressed against Vincent's thigh. Vincent slid his palm up Jasper's arm to the back of his neck, where he tangled his fingers in Jasper's hair and pulled him in for a quick kiss.

"Bend over," he murmured, nudging Jasper down to lie across his thighs. "And hands behind your back." He waited for Jasper to stop squirming and offer his hands, then secured a cuff around each wrist so his hands settled against the top of his ass. "Good boy." He dragged his fingertips down Jasper's spine as he found the remote with his other hand to start the action movie that was still queued up.

"Comfortable?" he asked, trading the remote for the lube.

"Yes, Sir," Jasper said, breathless and already sounding a bit desperate.

"Tell me if that changes." With that he poured lube directly over Jasper's ass crack. Jasper twitched with a sharp sound of surprise, and Vincent waited for him to still to start working his fingers in. He took his time, leisurely working in one finger and then a second and third during the first fifteen minutes of the movie. By the time he finally pressed the plug inside, Jasper was a panting, moaning mess of heated flesh.

He wiped his fingers off on the towel, then turned his attention to the movie as he caressed Jasper's ass and thighs. His other hand alternated between resting against Jasper's neck and tugging his hair.

Jasper let out a long pleading whine before going limp, his eyes closing and his breathing slowly evening out.

"Good boy," he murmured, flexing his fingers in Jasper's hair until he earned another moan. He let Jasper relax while he relished having his pet readily available. Even when he'd last had a sub, he'd rarely been able to indulge in such intimate touching outside of scenes.

"Did you enjoy wearing the fox ears?" he asked after a while, sliding his hand up to grope Jasper's ass. The immediate response was a strangled sound, which wasn't entirely surprising. Neither was the pink staining Jasper's neck and ears.

It was a long moment later before Jasper finally said, "It wasn't terrible."

Not what he'd hoped for. "But not good?" he prompted.

Jasper moved as if he was trying to sit up before slumping in defeat when his position and restraints made that impossible. "I wouldn't mind doing it again."

"Wouldn't mind?" Vincent asked dryly. "Did you hate it that much?"

"I didn't hate it," Jasper whispered, the pink darkening to red.

"No?"

"It was… weird."

Vincent hummed as he nudged and twisted the plug. "What part did you like about it?"

Jasper shifted enough to glance over his shoulder, briefly meeting Vincent's eye before smashing his face into the cushion so his words were muffled. "I liked that you liked it."

Vincent breathed through the burst of fondness in his chest and mussed Jasper's hair. "I've liked everything we've done."

"Yeah, but…." Jasper flexed his fingers, and when Vincent pressed his own hand against them Jasper latched on with a soft sigh. "You *really* liked it. You were all growly and possessive."

"And you like that?" he asked, lowering his voice and gripping Jasper's hip to tug him closer.

Jasper rocked onto his side to press back into Vincent's stomach. "Uh-huh. Makes me feel like you want me," he said, flicking his tongue out to wet his lips. "Like I'm welcome here."

"Of course you're welcome here," Vincent said. He gripped Jasper's arm to haul him upright so he could catch his lips in a kiss. "You're mine until you say otherwise."

"Yes, Sir," Jasper breathed, already curling his body into Vincent as he sought out another kiss, and then another, and Vincent lost track of the movie completely.

CHAPTER 4

JASPER ADJUSTED his suit for the umpteenth time as they headed into the performing arts center. He'd never been to a concert before, or was this considered a symphony? Violinist Ugetsu Kunihiko was his favorite artist and had been for the last several years. Jasper had found his music during his freshman year of high school, shortly after his brother moved out and left Jasper to deal with their drunken asshole of a father on his own.

He'd never told anyone that he'd contemplated taking his own life back then. The stress of school, of trying to find food in a house that rarely had more than booze, of the constant yelling and threats of violence. There'd been no reason to continue. No one would have missed him. His father kept a loaded gun in his dresser that Jasper had taken out at least twice, though he'd never been able to go through with it.

Then he'd heard someone listening to Ugetsu's music in the stairwell during lunch. He hadn't understood a word of the Japanese lyrics, but the dark violin music and soulful voice had stopped him in his tracks. He'd immediately searched the artist with an identifier app on his phone and spent the weekend downloading and listening to every song released, finding translations of the lyrics, and losing himself in the one thing he could focus on enough to pretend his life wasn't the shitty clusterfuck it was for a few hours each day.

Vincent's hand brushed against Jasper's, grounding him back in the here and now. In the hot summer evening and the sweet scent of the flowers blooming along the path. In the hotter press of Vincent's hand against his lower back as he guided Jasper into the building. In the sharp-yet-subtle scent of Vincent's cologne—spicy and woodsy and somehow the epitome of mind-blowing sex. Or maybe that was Jasper's bias; he liked how Vincent smelled.

And now he was utterly distracted for an entirely different reason.

He tilted his head into Vincent's shoulder and breathed deep with a soft moan. His eyes fluttered shut as he stepped closer, nearly tripping them both as his leg pressed into Vincent's with every step. Instead of pushing him away, Vincent slipped his hand from Jasper's back to his hip and held him there.

Jasper didn't even try to fight his grin as he wrapped his own arm around Vincent's waist. All his worries about tonight, whether they were overdressed or if Vincent would even enjoy this, became obsolete. He knew—hoped—Vincent would enjoy this because only an asshole with no musical taste at all couldn't appreciate it. And their clothes didn't matter. There were some in nice clothes, others dressed more casually, but Ugetsu's music meant more to him than being comfortable in old jeans and a T-shirt.

Vincent led the way to their seats. Bottom balcony, dead center of the stage. He'd have to thank Amber again; no way were these seats cheap.

They sat, and Jasper leaned forward, tucking his hands under his thighs as he scanned the theater, surprised but pleased to see it filling so quickly. He hadn't been sure what to expect since this wasn't a rock concert or big-name band. He tilted his head enough to glance at Vincent from the corner of his eye. His legs were crossed and he had his phone out, but Jasper leaned over enough to bump his shoulder against Vincent's arm.

"Thanks for bringing me here," he murmured. "You didn't have to."

Vincent slipped his phone into his pocket after silencing it and turned a mild frown on him. "Do I not owe you one date most weeks?"

Jasper shrugged. Sure, Vincent had put that in the new contract, but most of their dates so far had been dinner followed by some kind of scene. This was the first time they'd gone out as a couple that wasn't to the club or a restaurant. He'd been so excited over the concert itself that he hadn't realized that until now, and the burst of nerves in his stomach joined the others that had been growing since Vincent offered to take him away on a two-week vacation. Just them. Far enough away that no one could bother them or drag Vincent into work.

Starting tomorrow, he'd have Vincent completely to himself for fourteen days.

On one hand, *yessss*. On the other.... Holy shit, what if he fucked something up? Two weeks was a long time to be around someone. What if he got on Vincent's nerves? What if Vincent got on *his* nerves? He doubted that would happen. He really, really hoped that didn't happen, but it wasn't like they'd be having sex twenty-four seven. He'd at least learned that lesson early.

He blinked as Vincent grasped his chin and tipped his head back, his attention zeroing in on Vincent's dark hazel eyes that were focused on Jasper.

Vincent was silent for a beat before tracing his thumb beneath Jasper's lower lip. "I enjoy spending time with you."

Jasper's face heated, but he couldn't pull away. Not when Vincent had him trapped in that intense gaze of his. He wasn't used to being subjected to it outside of scenes.

Vincent traced his thumb back the other way, and Jasper couldn't help the shuddery breath as he tipped closer, hardly caring that they were in public. Not like they were being indecent, even if Vincent was watching him as if planning how to undress him and have his way with him.

A moan built in his throat that he couldn't quite stifle, and Vincent's eyes darkened before he flicked Jasper's nose and pulled his hand away. Which, unfair. He sat back with a huff. "You're not allowed to get me riled up in public," he muttered.

"No?" Vincent asked, amusement thick in his voice. "I don't recall that being in the contract."

Jasper wanted to say that it should be, but he couldn't make the words form. He refused to admit why as he shifted in his seat.

The lights flickered, and he turned his attention to the stage as the theater settled. The support orchestra finished setting up on one side, but his attention caught briefly on the man who sat at the piano before Ugetsu stepped onto the stage and applause rippled through the theater.

He practically vibrated in his seat with excitement as the lights dimmed. The moment Ugetsu put his bow to his violin, goose bumps burst across his arms and neck. Hearing this music through his headphones was one thing, but here, the rich violin music resonating and vibrating through the cool air directly from the source, was transcendental. The addition of a piano was new, but it worked to deepen and brighten the melody.

He closed his eyes for a long moment as he let the music crash over him. One song flowed into the next, and he pried his eyes open to watch, nearly falling out of his seat as he leaned forward as far as he could, transfixed by how such small adjustments of the bow changed the violin from remorseful to haunting. How the piano swelled and lifted it to hopeful. Ugetsu's rich voice melded with the music, its own counterpoint that sucked Jasper in even deeper.

He could have sat there listening forever, all the stress and anxiety and doubts melting away until all that was left was whatever feeling the music evoked in the moment, and Ugetsu was a master at evoking them all. From pits of despair so deep Jasper could see himself in his father's closet with a gun in his hands to regret so profound he could taste it on the back of his tongue to effervescent euphoria that left him breathless with yearning.

Two hours passed far too quickly, and Jasper couldn't quite comprehend it was over even as most of the audience surged to their feet in a standing ovation. He should get up and join them, but moving was beyond him at the moment. All he could do was sit and breathe as reality crashed back in around him.

Vincent's fingers in his hair worked to ground him, and he leaned into the touch with a deep sigh of pleasure. "Ready?" Vincent asked, still sitting despite those around them already slowly filing towards the exits.

"Mm, I guess." Vincent curled his fingers tighter but immediately released them, so quickly that Jasper could have believed he'd imagined it if not for the tingles along his scalp and the burst of heat in his gut. His hand found its way into Vincent's as they joined the procession, and he was almost scared to ask, "Did you enjoy it?"

"Yes." Vincent squeezed his hand, rubbing his thumb against the back of Jasper's. "Not nearly as much as you did, though. You seemed to be in a trance."

Jasper ducked his head and used the crowd as an excuse to press closer and hook his other hand beneath Vincent's arm. "I've never been to something like this."

"Do you want to do it again sometime?"

He jerked his head up in surprise. "Really?" He tried to keep the eager excitement under control but failed miserably.

Vincent glanced at him in obvious amusement and squeezed his hand again. "I'm sure we can find another we'd both enjoy."

Jasper grinned and didn't even try to hide the bounce in his step.

Getting out of the building took far longer than getting in, and the traffic wasn't any better, but it gave him time to come down from the high of seeing his favorite artist live. He was simultaneously buzzed and limp with catharsis, not unlike after an intense scene that pushed him into subspace.

By the time Vincent parked in the garage Jasper was yawning, his eyes drooping, and not even the knowledge that they'd be on a plane in a few hours could fully wake him up. He trudged upstairs where Vincent undressed him and tucked him into bed, and he sank into the deep sleep of the blissfully exhausted.

CHAPTER 5

MORNING CAME far too early in that it was still dark outside when their alarms went off. Vincent may have ensured they were properly packed the day before, but he couldn't help the need to double-check they had everything while Jasper made a quick breakfast of toast. He would have preferred a more substantial breakfast with several hours of flying ahead of them, but he didn't want to leave a mess that would sit for two weeks, and it was too early to stomach much of anything.

He'd paused his cleaning service and given his driver paid time off, starting the moment they were dropped at the airport. He wasn't entirely worried about forgetting something that couldn't be picked up at a local store, but he'd prefer not to have to make any detours.

He checked the drawers to grab a few more pairs of boxers and socks, just in case, and paused at the manilla envelopes tucked to the side. Their blood test results. He'd gotten them back weeks ago but hadn't bothered to bring them up since Jasper had been anxious about the changes they might bring. Maybe Vincent should have addressed it again when he'd first received them, but Jasper's exams had taken priority. And then the end of semester, Jasper's birthday, and this vacation.

Vincent grabbed the envelopes, tossed the extra clothes into his suitcase, tucked the test results into the front pouch, and zipped it up. Once he was sure he had his phone, wallet, and keys, he grabbed both their suitcases and rolled them out of the bedroom. He didn't dare risk breaking a limb by taking them both downstairs at once and by the time he had everything piled by the door, his driver was waiting at the curb.

"Ready?" he called, heading to the kitchen where Jasper had a piece of toast with melted peanut butter waiting on a plate for him.

Jasper shoved the last bit of his own toast in his mouth. "Yup!" he said brightly, rinsing his plate before quickly leaning in to plant a kiss on Vincent's cheek. "I'll get the bags," he said, already out of the kitchen.

Vincent grimaced at the greasy residue from a smear of peanut butter Jasper left behind. "Damn brat," he muttered under his breath. He folded his toast in half and ate it in a few bites, drained a glass of water, and headed after Jasper, making sure all the lights were off as he went.

He grabbed his laptop bag and was about to lock up when Jasper raced back inside, muttering about his phone charger. Vincent shook his head and waited the few seconds it took for Jasper to return. "Got everything?"

"Think so."

Vincent locked up and put his bag in the trunk with the rest as Jasper shoved his charger into a suitcase, and then they were on the road.

The sun was breaking over the horizon when they reached the airport, and half an hour later they were at their gate with less than an hour before boarding. Jasper sat next to him, shifting in his seat every other second, his leg bouncing as if caffeine had replaced his blood supply.

Since nothing Vincent could say would ease Jasper's nerves about flying for the first time, he wrapped his hand around Jasper's fingers instead and squeezed.

Jasper heaved a deep sigh and slumped against Vincent's side despite the uncomfortable arm rest between them. A long moment of silence passed before Jasper bumped his elbow against Vincent. "Sooo do you have any wicked plans for me tonight?"

"Settling in and making dinner," Vincent replied, scrolling through the list on his phone one last time to make sure he hadn't forgotten anything. When Jasper bit his shoulder, he set his phone aside and flicked the brat's nose. "And punishing you if you keep that up," he added dryly.

Jasper pulled back with a grin. "Promise?"

Vincent laughed. "Absolutely not," he said, not about to encourage Jasper to be even more of a brat, even if his enthusiasm was welcomed. Considering how out of his depth Jasper had been a few months ago, it was nice to see him finding things he knew he liked.

"I thought vacations were supposed to be *enjoyable*," Jasper huffed.

"It will be. You'll have to be patient." Vincent would have to be patient too, since the thought of having full access to Jasper for more than a few days at a time was enough to give him all kinds of ideas. More intense scenes, testing Jasper's limits, exploring things they hadn't tried yet. Two weeks was nothing in the grand scheme of things, but it felt like the beginning of a small eternity.

Getting settled on the plane was easy enough as he'd booked first class. Jasper lasted a whole two minutes before he piped up, "I almost expected you to have a private plane."

Vincent hesitated a moment before admitting, "I wasn't sure you wouldn't freak out," and braced himself as Jasper whipped his head around from staring out the window to staring at him in shock.

"You have one?"

"Technically it belongs to Arthur, my grandfather, but I can request access easily enough."

"Unbelievable," Jasper murmured. "Is your entire family rich?"

Vincent sighed, unable to control his wince. "Not exactly," he replied slowly. A plane wasn't exactly the best place to have such a personal conversation, but they had a few hours with nothing better to do than get to know each other when sex wasn't a viable option. So he explained how his mother became estranged from her parents when she got pregnant out of wedlock and ran away to the US with his father, who had died before Vincent was born. It was only after his mother's death that his grandparents were notified of her passing and became involved in Vincent's life.

His grandmother Valencia wasn't keen on him leeching off the family name, but Arthur refused to sever ties with his only grandchild. Vincent's second cousin on his grandmother's side had been set to inherit the full Thornwell fortune, but with Vincent's latest business successes, there'd been mention of changing his grandfather's part of the inheritance to Vincent.

As far as he understood, Valencia was part of an old Davenport lineage, with her older brother's children to inherit their family legacy, while Vincent's great-grandfather and grandfather had made their own fortune.

"Isn't that going to make you a target for the rest of the family?"

"Possibly," he replied dryly. While he appreciated that Arthur was likely trying to make up for abandoning them, part of Vincent still wanted to refuse his help as a matter of principle. Thanks to his numerous years of therapy, he knew that stemmed from some lingering desire to remain in solidarity with his mother. She'd never spoken about her parents other than to say she'd been disowned for going against their wishes, and as far as he knew, she never reached out to them.

Vincent hadn't had much choice but to accept Arthur's help when he'd been in the hospital and facing charges. Then finishing college in Europe had been a given as he'd been in his grandfather's debt from both medical and legal bills. Now he was on stable ground again, with plenty of money of his own. He kept in contact because he genuinely liked Arthur, though Valencia acted as if she hated his guts.

He glanced at his hand as Jasper threaded their fingers together and squeezed. "All that to say most of my family might be ridiculously wealthy, but I wasn't raised with the access to it that I have now."

"That explains a lot," Jasper said but didn't elaborate, merely offered a cheeky smile when Vincent eyed him. "What about your father's family?"

"Never met any of them." He'd never tried finding them either, especially while in Europe, in case it pushed his grandmother over the edge. He didn't even know what the man looked like. His mother had no pictures of him. All Vincent had was the simple wedding band that had never been worn as his father died before they could have an actual wedding.

"I don't really remember my mom," Jasper offered after a long moment of silence, his voice soft.

Vincent tightened his fingers around Jasper's. "What do you remember?"

"Her laugh.... She would cackle and start snorting and couldn't stop," he said with a faint smile, but he didn't continue.

"What happened?"

Jasper sighed and let his head thunk against Vincent's shoulder. "She died. I was five or six. She got dizzy at work and fell. Died on the way to the hospital."

Vincent blew out a breath. "That's why you chose to become an EMT?"

Jasper shrugged. "Maybe. I don't know. By the time I was old enough to understand what really happened to her, there was no one around I could ask about it."

"Even Amber?"

"They basically abandoned us," he said, a bitter anger in his words. "We never saw her or her family outside of holidays anyway, and Dad stopped taking us after Mom died."

"Is that when he started drinking?" Vincent was starting to piece together a better picture of Jasper's life before now, and it was worse than he'd initially thought.

"Yeah," he whispered, his fingers limp in Vincent's grasp.

Vincent stroked his own against them before lifting Jasper's hand to brush his lips across his knuckles, then he pulled out his earbuds and his phone to connect to the Wi-Fi and let Jasper pick a show to watch. They spent the flight watching the new Star Wars series, only getting through most of the second episode before they landed.

They made a quick restroom stop, then found their bags and the car rental counter, and by the time they got loaded up, it was lunchtime. "It's about an hour drive from here. Hungry?"

Jasper sank into the passenger seat with a wrinkle of his nose. "I can wait until we get there."

Vincent gave him a dubious look. "Why don't we stop and get a snack at least." He found the nearest gas station, got them set with drinks and snacks, and put in the address for the cabins. Jasper was asleep before they made it out of the city, which wasn't surprising considering the ungodly hour they'd been up at. He used the chance to call Zach.

"Oh? Two calls in as many weeks? Don't I feel special," Zach answered.

"Careful, I might start to believe you actually miss talking to me," Vincent replied dryly.

Zach snorted. "Oh, the horror. You on the way, then?"

"Just got on the road. When were you wanting to do dinner?"

"I figured you'd want to settle in and enjoy your new sub first. Get all those pent-up kinky itches scratched properly. How's Wednesday or Thursday sound?"

"Works for me."

"Great. Don't bother with stopping by the office. I'll go unlock the cabin before you get here and leave the key and paperwork there. Make sure to read and sign everything," Zach said, stressing the last bit in a serious yet pleading tone. "It's the second left after the office. It'll have the green porch."

"Aww, preferential treatment? For me?"

"You're right. I'll have to leave a little special something on your pillow to balance that out."

"Don't you dare," Vincent growled, but the call disconnected before he even got the words out. He muttered under his breath and questioned whatever life decisions he'd made that meant most of his friends were brats or dicks.

The drive passed in silence, and he used the time to center himself and consider the different scenes he had in mind. To move his focus from work and everyday tasks to being the Dom Jasper needed and deserved for the next two weeks.

THE CITY fell away around them, slowly replaced with the large trees of deep woods. Eventually Vincent spotted the sign advertising the cabin exit in five miles. A completely unassuming wooden sign with fancy script, only the coiled loop of rope hooked over one corner giving any indication of the type of clientele they catered to.

He took the exit and followed the road to a small office building with a Welcome to Evergreen Escape sign out front. He continued on, following Zach's instructions until he found the cabin with the green porch and parked. Then he reached over and gently shook Jasper's shoulder. "Jas, wake up. We're here."

Jasper stirred with a groaned protest before jolting upright, somehow going from dead asleep to excited in point five seconds. He stared at the cabin with wide eyes before hopping out and up the few steps to get inside the cabin before Vincent could even turn the car off.

He shook his head and got the bags, then dumped them inside the door before turning and taking in the mix of rustic log cabin and modern design. The main floor was divided by a large sofa and wall-mounted TV to the left and dining table to the right, a doorway leading to the kitchen beyond it. Stairs near the far wall led up to a loft, where he could see the king-size bed to the right and a walled-off section he assumed was the bathroom on the left.

Since he didn't see Jasper anywhere, he headed down the hall and found him standing inside the playroom. He let out a low whistle at the size of it. Pictures didn't do the cabins justice.

Nearly double the size of his own, with one corner set up as a shower with frosted glass walls for easy cleanup. The room was divided into sections, one dedicated to suspension, another to impact play with a bench much like the ones he had at the club. The benches were custom-made by Zach, and Vincent had ordered all of the ones in the club and at home from Zach when he'd first started planning the club.

One corner of the playroom even had one of the exam tables he'd seen on the website meant for medical scenes. Several shelves lined one wall, full of candles, a violet wand, and what looked like a fire kit. Most of the toys were in new unopened packages, and anything they used would be theirs to keep and charged to his account after they left.

Jasper made a sound somewhere between a laugh and a gurgle. "This is insane."

Vincent raised an eyebrow, hooking an arm around Jasper's waist. "Is this not why you picked this place?"

"I mean, yeah, but…." He flapped a hand at the room. "You don't even have all this."

"A few of the private rooms at the club have a lot of it," he said. Except for the extensive medical paraphernalia. He'd been considering setting one up, but after the unfortunate scalpel incident at the club, he was having second thoughts. "Why don't you take the bags up while I make a late lunch."

Jasper eyed the room one last time before following Vincent back to the door to grab the bags.

Vincent continued into the kitchen. Zach had sent pictures of the grocery delivery and confirmed everything had arrived, so he grabbed one of the packages of chicken and some broccoli from the fridge to start on a quick stir-fry. He'd barely gotten the chicken opened when a loud "Holy fuck!" came from the loft.

He stepped out of the kitchen to find Jasper clutching the railing at the top of the stairs. "What's wrong?"

"There's a giant spider on the bed."

Vincent grimaced and made a note to strangle Zach. "It's probably fake," he said and sighed when Jasper turned an incredulous look on him.

"Why would it be fake?"

"Because Zach is an asshole and knows I hate spiders."

"Makes sense you'd be friends," Jasper murmured.

Vincent ignored that and went back to cooking. It wasn't until he'd finished up that he noticed Jasper hadn't joined him. He set the skillet aside to keep warm and went in search of his wayward brat, only to find him sitting on the edge of the bed with a familiar manila envelope in his hands.

When Vincent sat next to him, he tensed. "I wasn't snooping," he said quickly. "I was trying to find my charger."

"I didn't think you were," Vincent said, holding his hand out and taking the papers when Jasper offered them. He hadn't opened either envelope when they first arrived, and he hadn't doubted Jasper when he said he was clean, but it was a relief to see it verified. He wasn't worried about his own so he opened the other envelope, quickly glanced over it to make sure it said the same, and handed it to Jasper.

When he stayed silent, Vincent took the papers back and slipped them into their respective envelopes. "Like I said before, this changes nothing unless you want it to."

Jasper gripped the covers on either side of his legs. "I don't know…."

"Then it changes nothing," Vincent said firmly, turning to face Jasper directly and stifling a sigh at his dubious expression. He grasped Jasper's chin to tilt his head up and force him to meet his eye. "We'll continue using protection until you say otherwise." Then he pressed Jasper back to lie down.

Jasper huffed as his back hit the bed, but he lifted his arms to rest above his head as if by habit. Vincent let out a soft hum of approval and stretched out over him, sliding his hand up Jasper's chest before tipping his head back and indulging in a kiss. He took his time with it, kissing Jasper until his breaths came faster and soft pleading moans escaped. When he pulled back, Jasper whined.

"You're not going to fuck me now, are you?"

Vincent laughed. "No."

"Whyyyy?"

He slipped a hand under Jasper's shirt and slid along warm skin until he found a nipple, pitching his voice lower as he answered. "We have two weeks, and I intend to make the most of it." Then he pulled his hand away and stood. "And I have a list of options for how to spend our time here that you need to go through. Which can wait until after we eat."

He pulled away and headed back to the kitchen, snorting softly when Jasper whined and grumbled behind him. They had two weeks. No way was he going to rush or skip the planning. Besides, Jasper enjoyed the teasing as much as he did.

He dished up the stir-fry and passed a plate to Jasper, and if they ate a bit quicker than usual, he pretended not to notice.

When they headed back to the loft, he lifted the suitcase onto the dresser, found his notebook, and flipped to the page with what he'd listed out before handing it to Jasper. A pen was tucked into the spiral. "Circle the ones you're most interested in. Cross out the ones that are limits. Would you prefer to look them over alone?"

Jasper stared at the page for long enough that Vincent worried he'd broken him, but he finally croaked, "You can stay." He stretched out on the bed and rolled to his stomach as he snatched a pillow to lie on.

Vincent settled beside him, nudging Jasper's shirt up enough to rest a hand at the small of his back while he nuzzled against Jasper's neck.

"You're distracting me," Jasper said, his eye roll audible.

Vincent answered with a bite against his shoulder. "Good."

Jasper huffed, but he gamely focused on the notebook, crossing a few options out as he obviously did a quick skim. It wasn't until he started circling things that Vincent focused more on the notebook and Jasper's answers than on distracting his brat.

CHAPTER 6

JASPER READ the list several times as he slowly marked things off. It wasn't until the fourth time he circled something that he noticed how Vincent's fingers flexed against his hip when he did so. He side-eyed Vincent as a small thrill of power went through him. Knowing Vincent was interested in everything on the paper he was tempted to circle all of it, but he had to remind himself that wasn't what Vincent wanted.

Still, it was a heady sensation. He was still finding his footing with the knowledge that so much of what they did together started and ended with Jasper's choices, but this was a blatant reminder of how much power he truly held in the relationship.

Vincent raised an eyebrow when he noticed Jasper staring. "Problem?"

He grinned and leaned in to peck Vincent's lips. "Just thinking." Vincent didn't appear convinced, but that was fine. It was more fun if he was kept guessing. Jasper turned back to the list, hesitating at *humiliation* and tapping it with the end of the pen. "What exactly does this entail?"

Vincent propped his chin on Jasper's shoulder. "That would depend on you," he said and squeezed Jasper's hip before he could draw breath to protest. "You enjoy being called slut," he murmured, and Jasper shivered as heat tightened his gut. "We could explore that some more if you're interested." He chuckled as Jasper circled it twice.

Jasper continued through the last few he hadn't marked yet and tapped *predicament bondage*. "What's this?"

"Restraining someone so they have a specific, limited range of movement or positions."

"How's that different from how you usually tie me up?"

Vincent smiled briefly and nipped Jasper's earlobe. "Usually I like to pair it with a set of instructions."

Jasper refused to be distracted by Vincent's lips and teeth and warm breath even if it was nearly impossible not to be. "Instructions that I can follow?"

"If you try hard enough, maybe."

Jasper huffed and slanted Vincent his best unimpressed stare, glad he was on his stomach since he was thoroughly worked up at the mere thought of experiencing anything on the page. "Is this one of those particular tastes you mentioned?"

"Yes."

He eyed the list and wondered what else on there fell into that category. Most of it he'd at least heard of even if he'd never thought to try it out or assumed he wouldn't like it. Like CBT. But Vincent made it easy to say yes to almost everything. Maybe that was stupid of him, willingly jumping into anything Vincent wanted to do to him, but Vincent hadn't given him a reason not to trust him so far, so he circled predicament bondage.

He tilted his head as he reached role-play, and he didn't miss the way Vincent stilled beside him. He glanced over curiously. "What kind of role-play?" he asked before remembering Vincent explaining how he realized he was into the whole kink thing. "Like playing doctor?" he asked brightly. The heat in Vincent's gaze in response to that question left him momentarily dizzy.

"Yes," Vincent said, voice rough enough to make him shiver.

Jasper leaned closer with a soft, "You want to do naughty things to your patient?" Vincent's breath audibly hitched, and Jasper bit his lip to keep from grinning. "You want to give me a prostate exam with your *penis*?" he asked in a scandalized whisper. He couldn't help the burst of triumphant satisfaction in his chest when Vincent rolled away with a spluttered laugh. "Sir!" he gasped. "That is *not* appropriate medical practice!"

"Oh yes, how could I forget," Vincent replied dryly. "You're the medical expert. Maybe you should be the doctor."

Jasper's eyes widened as he pictured himself giving Vincent a prostate exam with his penis. He didn't often imagine himself as the one on top and wasn't sure he should even be entertaining the idea since a sub couldn't top. Right?

Vincent settled on his side and propped his head on his fist, reaching up to brush Jasper's hair out of his eyes. "Pet?"

Jasper blinked and focused on the notebook again, but Vincent wasn't having it. He buried a hand in Jasper's hair and turned his head to face him again.

"What are you thinking?"

He flushed as a soft sound of protest escaped, though he stopped himself from saying ”nothing.” “I don’t want to say.”

Vincent raised an eyebrow, and for a moment Jasper expected him to demand an answer anyway, but he let go.

Jasper swallowed and turned back to the notebook, hesitating before circling role-play, along with the others he hadn’t crossed out, before handing it over. “All done,” he said. “Now what?”

“Now,” Vincent said as he tugged the notebook closer and studied Jasper’s choices, “we enjoy ourselves for the next few days before Zach insists on meeting you.”

Jasper rolled onto his side and hooked a leg over Vincent’s hip. “The one who owns this place?”

“Mm-hmm. One of the owners. He makes most of the benches and furniture I have in the club.”

“And he wants to meet me? Why?”

Vincent gave him an exasperated look. “Because I’ve taken you on as my sub.”

Jasper wiggled his fingers into the top of Vincent’s pants, biting back a grin when Vincent let him. “He’s not going to give me a shovel talk, is he?”

Vincent snorted and slid his hand down to cup Jasper’s ass. “If anything, I expect him to tell you to find someone better.”

“I’m starting to see a pattern with your friends, Sir,” he murmured, though when Vincent pressed closer and fastened his lips to Jasper’s neck, he couldn’t have said what day it was, much less voice a fleeting thought of Vincent’s friends all being dicks.

“You’ll probably like Aston better, then,” Vincent murmured between kisses as he moved down Jasper’s throat.

“Uh-huh.”

“He’s the one who took all the photos hanging in the club.”

Jasper blinked as his brain caught up with the fact Vincent wasn’t kissing him anymore and was instead staring down at him with a considering expression. “Pictures,” he repeated, the word feeling like nonsense on his tongue. He swallowed the whine building at the back of his throat. Why were they still talking when they could be having sex?

The pictures in the club. The black-and-white portraits of people in various poses that lined the walls. Most of them naked or at least showing a lot of skin. Vincent had said he'd hang a picture of Jasper if he let him, but that was only talk. Right?

"You want a picture of me?" he asked, eyeing Vincent warily when he nodded. "Why would you want a picture of me hanging in the club?"

"Various reasons," Vincent replied, sliding a hand under Jasper's shirt and circling a finger around his nipple. "I did warn you I was a voyeur."

Jasper swallowed a moan and valiantly fought to stay focused. "You do-don't need a picture for that."

"Maybe I want the reminder. Or the simple pleasure of having a framed portrait of you submitting for me." He punctuated the comment with a quick pinch and tug on Jasper's nipple, and that was the end of Jasper's battle.

None of the photos in the club had faces. If Vincent wanted to add one of Jasper to the wall, he didn't really mind. It was kinda hot actually. Jasper knew he wasn't much to look at. No muscles from working out, much less a cut physique, but apparently Vincent liked something about him enough to immortalize in a picture.

"Okay." He tugged Vincent close enough to nip his lower lip. "*Now* can we have sex?"

Vincent huffed a laugh against Jasper's cheek. "Insatiable."

"Your fault, Sir." He worked his shirt over his head then sprawled out on the bed. "You need to take responsibility. I expect mind-blowing sex at *least* once a day while we're here."

"Oh, how will I ever meet such demanding… demands."

Jasper grinned. "Such eloquent eloquence, Sir. You really have a way with words. Really swept me off my fe-eeet!" he squeaked, rolling away with a laugh when Vincent retaliated by pinching his side. He tried to crawl away, but Vincent easily pinned him down, and when Vincent's lips traced a path down his spine, he gave up trying to get away altogether.

Chapter 7

Jasper lazed in bed after he woke, his excitement returning tenfold with consciousness. He was officially on vacation. With Vincent.

He rolled over to find Vincent still asleep and leaned in to press a light kiss to his cheek before climbing out of bed. When he made it to the kitchen to start breakfast, he was surprised by all the food in the fridge, though he probably shouldn't have been. If Vincent knew the owners, he was likely getting all kinds of perks. Even the coffee was the same kind as the one Vincent had at home, and he rolled his eyes as he started a pot.

He put some music on his phone and started scrambling eggs with bacon. Vincent finally joined him when he was finishing up and sleepily nuzzled into his neck. Jasper tipped his head back with a grin. "What's the plan for today?"

Vincent tightened his arms with a hum and kissed across Jasper's neck and shoulders. "Hiking."

"Sex first?" he pleaded, bumping his ass into Vincent's groin.

Vincent groped him and stole a piece of bacon before filling a cup of coffee. "Maybe."

"Maybe, my ass," he grumbled under his breath, trudging out of the cabin after Vincent, but his disappointment faded quickly as they followed a path into the woods.

There were no sounds of the city. No cars honking or zooming past. No people shouting. No stench of exhaust. He breathed deep and tipped his head back as he listened to the birds and insects. It was still early enough it wasn't too hot, and a cool breeze rustled through the leaves. He'd never seen so much green before.

The path was packed dirt and rocks, winding through the trees until it branched in three directions. A sign pointed out a lake to the left, hot springs in the center, and a recreation center and main office to the right.

Vincent headed left, and Jasper took the chance to thread their fingers together and lean into Vincent's side.

"Where's the zip lining?"

"It's a separate business that they partnered with a few miles from here."

"Does that mean we can't go?"

Vincent let out a groan but quickly cut it off. "You really want to go?"

"Yeah, it sounds fun."

"I'll work it into the schedule."

"Oh, is there an actual schedule?" Jasper asked, tipping his head back with a laugh. "Is it a list of all the positions you want to have sex in?"

"And all the ways I intend to torment you," Vincent added dryly.

"Can I see?"

"Absolutely not."

Jasper huffed and pressed his face against Vincent's shoulder before biting.

"Starting to think I should put a muzzle on you."

Jasper smirked. "Woof."

The lake came into view a few minutes later, the water still and clear enough to see straight to the bottom. No one else was around as they wandered to the edge of the water. "We going for a swim?"

"You can."

Jasper rolled his eyes and bumped into Vincent. "What'd you pack the swim trunks for, then?"

Vincent bumped back before turning to walk along the water's edge. "The hot springs."

Well, at least he'd get to see Vincent mostly naked and wet at some point. Maybe he'd even get a chance to finally see him fully naked, scars and all. He stopped to pick up a few rocks and turned them over in his hand. "Can you skip rocks?" he asked, rubbing dirt off one that seemed promising, even if he had no idea what one should look like. It was mostly flat; that was all he knew to search for.

Vincent glanced back at him. "Never tried."

"Me neither." Jasper tossed the rock up to test the weight of it, then turned to the water and let it fly. It skipped once before disappearing with a *sploosh*. Huffing, he dropped the other rocks and searched for more until he found some better ones, though even after four attempts he could only get one skip out of them.

When he noticed Vincent was simply standing and watching him, he offered one of the rocks he'd found. Vincent eyed it dubiously but took it, then stared at it as he turned it over and over in his hand. After a long moment he sighed and turned to the water. When he threw the rock it sailed several feet into the air and plunked straight into the lake.

"Try lower," Jasper offered, holding out another rock and wiggling it when Vincent made no move to take it. "One more?" he asked. "If you make it skip I'll give you a massage?"

"Why are you bribing me to skip a rock?"

Jasper shrugged. "You said flattery won't work on you."

Vincent shook his head, though Jasper was sure he caught an amused smile before Vincent turned away. He wiped the dirt off the rock, bent to rinse it in the water, tossed it in the air a few times, and finally drew his arm back. This time he threw it close to the water's surface, where it did a tiny bounce before plunking to the bottom.

"Close enough," Jasper said, dropping his last rock in favor of taking Vincent's hand.

"You're very easy to please."

"It's not like it's an entirely selfless offer," he said quietly. He couldn't give Vincent a decent massage if he was dressed. Maybe he'd even give Vincent a happy ending, without a condom. He'd read their test results. They were both clean. Was there really any reason to keep using protection? He wasn't going to cheat on Vincent, and he trusted Vincent wouldn't cheat on him.

Even when Vincent did the occasional scene with subs in the club, he said he never had sex with them. Jasper had seen firsthand how true that was. He'd offered to let Vincent fuck him more than once their first couple of scenes together, and Vincent never took him up on it.

The day was warming up by the time they left the lake and returned to the cooler shade of the trees. Thankfully Vincent led them back to the cabin rather than explore further. Once they were inside and rehydrated, Jasper hooked his arms around Vincent's waist. "Massage?"

"I have a better idea." Vincent slipped his hand from Jasper's back to his ass and squeezed. "Why don't we try some predicament bondage?"

The heat and arousal that went straight to Jasper's cock was almost painful in its intensity. "Yes, please."

"Strip and wait by the patio door," Vincent ordered, then headed down the hall towards the playroom.

Jasper toed his socks off and kicked them to the side, the rest of his clothes following a moment later. Only when he was by the door did he realize it overlooked part of the hiking trail they'd used. The chances of someone wandering close to their cabin were slim, but not zero. The papers they'd signed mentioned the explicit nature of the resort, and that by staying they agreed to the possibility of seeing others in various states of undress or involved in scenes, sexual or otherwise.

He'd never considered being watched before, at least not outside of the club, but Vincent had kept their scenes private. Either in a room at the club or at home. Did Vincent want to show him off? That possibility sent an interesting thrill through him, even more than the fact that Vincent apparently wanted to put a tastefully nude portrait of Jasper on display.

He turned when Vincent joined him, his gaze snagging on the leather cuffs. He wasn't sure what he'd expected, but cuffs seemed too simple for something called predicament bondage. "Is that it?"

"No," Vincent said but didn't elaborate. Instead he pressed the fingertips of his free hand to Jasper's stomach and backed him against the door.

The cool glass against his skin made him shiver, but Vincent's lips on his warmed him quickly, and when Vincent ordered him to turn and put his hands behind his back, nerves and excitement heated him even further. A soft moan escaped him when the cuffs were secured, and he caught Vincent's smug expression in the reflection as he let his forehead rest against the glass.

Vincent put a hand beside his head, but it took a moment for him to notice the quarter beneath Vincent's finger. "Here's the predicament," Vincent murmured, his low voice in Jasper's ear sending goose bumps all down his arms. "Hold the coin against the glass with your nose. If you let it fall, you don't get to come."

"What?"

"Can you do that?"

It sounded easy enough, and he wasn't about to back down now. "Yes, Sir."

Vincent chuckled. Maybe it was Jasper's imagination, but it sounded skeptical. He wondered what he'd missed, but he'd be fine. Even if he dropped the quarter, he was sure he'd still enjoy whatever Vincent had planned. Maybe more so.

Vincent moved the quarter close enough for Jasper to press his nose against. Almost immediately he realized this was a trap. Without his hands he couldn't balance, and he was forced to smush his nose against the glass along with his forehead to ensure he didn't let the coin fall. Keeping the quarter from moving took enough focus that he didn't realize Vincent was putting a cock ring on him until it was secured, and then Vincent gripped Jasper's hips and kissed down his spine.

That was mildly distracting, but Jasper managed to keep his face and the quarter against the glass. At least until Vincent sank to his knees and spread Jasper's cheeks, followed by hot breath between them. Shock and disbelief shivered through him. Vincent had never even given him a blow job without a condom in place. Surely he wouldn't—

The moment Vincent's tongue touched him, Jasper's entire body jerked as if he'd been shocked. He rocked onto his toes with a sharp, eager moan, his breath fogging the glass. When that delicious heat and pressure vanished and Vincent *tsk*ed, Jasper realized his nose wasn't pressed against the glass anymore, and the quarter was nowhere to be found.

"Shit," he gasped, slumping against the door with a whine.

Vincent slid his body against Jasper's as he stood. "I take it you truly understand now?" he murmured, dark amusement in his voice.

"Such a dick, Sir."

"You like it." Vincent pressed the quarter to the glass and slid it closer to bump against Jasper's nose. "You can have one more chance. Do you still think you can do it?"

"Not if you put your tongue on me again," he grumbled.

"Pity. Here." Vincent bumped the coin against his nose again.

Once Jasper was settled, he focused on breathing and staying still and not on the sound of the lube popping open, which worked up until Vincent had two fingers inside him. Then he was screwed. Figuratively and innuendoly.

The glass fogged to the point he couldn't see anything, and the condensation made it slippery. Somehow he managed to keep the quarter in place, even when Vincent slid both hands up Jasper's chest and tormented his nipples for what seemed like hours. As much as he wanted to give in to the pleasure and simply enjoy whatever Vincent wanted to do with him, he had to keep the coin from falling.

It wasn't even about getting off at the end at that point. He'd already dropped it once, and Vincent let him have a second chance. He couldn't fail again.

Then Vincent ripped open a condom a moment before his zipper rasped open. Jasper braced himself as best he could but still couldn't keep his body from arching in pleasure as Vincent pushed inside him.

The coin slipped, but he caught it with his lips, which made it hard to breathe when he was already gasping for air.

"Good boy," Vincent murmured in Jasper's ear, sliding his hands over Jasper's chest and tweaking his nipples again. "But can you keep it there?"

He attempted to answer, but it came out as muffled nonsense, then turned into a long moan when Vincent began thrusting. Slow enough not to pull Jasper away from the glass, hard enough he was forced onto the balls of his feet to keep steady. The chafe of the cuffs was almost pleasant but too distracting on top of everything else.

The glass became slick from his desperate breaths. The quarter slipped, and he caught it with his chin, but it was no use. He couldn't properly enjoy himself when he couldn't move freely. Or as freely as his restraints allowed.

As he pushed back to meet Vincent's next thrust, his head slipped down and his chin came away from the glass far enough for the coin to fall free. He whimpered softly but with almost as much relief as disappointment.

Behind him Vincent froze, then pressed forward to pin Jasper bodily against the door with a soft *tsk*. "Looks like you won't be getting off."

Jasper didn't care. Not when he could finally focus on Vincent taking him apart. "Shut up and fuck me, Sir," he gasped, pushing his hips back with a pleading moan.

Vincent took the hint like the good Dom he was, and Jasper bit his lip against a delirious laugh as he fought the urge to call Vincent a good Dom like Vincent called him a good boy. Vincent gripped Jasper's hip, his other arm braced against the window beside Jasper's head, breath coming in hot puffs against his shoulder as Vincent took his pleasure.

Jasper splayed and flexed his fingers, managing to latch on to Vincent's shirt with louder moans to urge him on. He might not get to come, but somehow that made this even hotter, knowing Vincent was fucking him because Vincent wanted to and not because Jasper had begged for it. He closed his eyes with a groan, muttering taunts and pleas alike under his breath until Vincent bit his shoulder with a breathless laugh and came.

Neither of them moved for a long moment, Vincent standing with his forehead resting on Jasper's shoulder while he was trapped against the door. Finally Vincent straightened and pulled out, his hands lingering against Jasper's hips like a caress.

"Good boy," he murmured, pressing a lingering kiss to Jasper's neck before stepping away.

He might not have gotten off, but satiation made his aching arousal bearable. Apparently… he liked being used? He'd dabbled in it before when Vincent gave him a taste of being punished, but this was more intense. Probably from the risk of being seen by someone. Not that it mattered.

Once Vincent cleaned him up and released him, he found the notebook with the list and snagged a pen to circle *slave for a day* twice.

CHAPTER 8

VINCENT STARED at his book, though he'd given up on reading a while ago, his stomach a twisted heartburn mess of excitement and nerves. He'd hoped it would settle once they had a proper scene and found their footing here, but it only intensified when he'd seen what Jasper had circled yesterday.

Part of him worried their scenes were escalating in intensity too fast to be sustainable, but most of that was Jasper discovering new things that he enjoyed. Even by his own standards he didn't think anything they'd tried up to now was extreme or intense, except maybe when he'd tied Jasper to the coffee table.

Vincent had kept his own fetishes to himself so far, and he'd hoped to introduce Jasper to at least one or two during their time here. He'd wanted to try some role-play with something simple, maybe a tacky porno setup like a pizza delivery or plumber, but leave it to Jasper to mention a doctor scene. He wasn't exactly surprised that Jasper remembered his comment about his first inclination for kink, but he certainly wasn't prepared for his reaction to it.

As much as Vincent wanted to delve into medical role-play, he didn't want to scare Jasper off, but now he couldn't get it out of his head. And with the medical chair *right there* calling to him from the playroom….

Jasper shifted on the couch next to him, and Vincent welcomed the distraction. He'd learned Jasper's mannerisms well enough by now to know Jasper was thinking of asking for something. He ran his fingers through Jasper's hair before resting his hand on the inside of his thigh. Jasper shivered and pressed his face against Vincent's arm, where he proceeded to gnaw briefly like an irritated cat.

"Problem?" he asked dryly, finally giving up on pretending to read his book.

"No." Jasper nuzzled against the spot he'd been biting before tipping his head back. "Can we try something?"

"Probably."

He rolled his eyes but wasn't deterred. "Can you…? Do you know what kabedon is?"

It sounded vaguely familiar, but Vincent couldn't pinpoint why. "I don't think so."

Jasper bit his lower lip before rolling off the couch, keeping hold of Vincent's arm and tugging as he got to his feet.

Vincent set his book aside and indulged him as he followed Jasper to the nearest wall with space enough for them to stand.

"So you put a hand on the wall and… lean in menacingly."

He raised an eyebrow and managed to keep a straight face. "Menacingly."

Jasper flushed and flapped a hand. "Like, intimidating."

He hummed softly, pleased Jasper was asking for something but also in a mood to return the usual bratty attitude. He stretched his arm out to press his hand to the wall, then kept his body stiff as he leaned towards Jasper. "Like this?"

With a huff, Jasper planted both hands against Vincent's chest and pushed him back. "No. More… threatening."

Vincent shifted a step to the side as he leaned in, deliberately loosening his stance as if coming up to talk to a close friend. "Better?"

"Now you're being a dick," Jasper muttered and pushed him away again. "Forget it."

He caught Jasper with a hand against his chest when he tried to walk away and roughly shoved him against the wall as he slammed his other palm above Jasper's head. He leaned in with a low chuckle, sliding his hand up Jasper's chest to rest against his throat.

Jasper squeaked and grasped Vincent's arm as his breathing turned ragged, his body slipping a bit against the wall as if his legs tried to give out.

"Is this what you wanted, pet?" he whispered, noting Jasper's dilated pupils and the rapid pulse beneath his fingers.

"Uh-huh," Jasper wheezed, tipping his head back with a soft moan.

Vincent nuzzled his cheek, then traced his tongue along the shell of Jasper's ear before biting it. "You want to be menaced?" he asked, wedging a thigh between Jasper's legs. He pressed a thumb beneath his jaw, forcing his chin up farther as he dragged his nose across Jasper's cheek and kissed the tip of his nose.

Then he straightened and stepped back as he dropped his hand, only for Jasper to keep hold of his sleeve with a dazed expression.

After a moment Jasper collected himself enough to pout at Vincent, though it quickly morphed into a challenging lift of his chin. "You call that menacing?"

Vincent stifled a laugh and settled for tilting his head as he stepped into Jasper's space again. He caught both of Jasper's wrists and forced them up over his head, pinning them against the wall and holding them with one hand. With his other he traced a fingertip down Jasper's throat as he eyed the button-up shirt. One he'd bought when he went on a quick supply run for this vacation. He'd picked up several cheap shirts for the both of them for this trip, so he wasn't worried about replacing it. Grabbing the center, he ripped it open with enough force to send the buttons flying.

Jasper yelped in surprise and instinctively tried to pull his wrists free, but Vincent tightened his grip to nearly bruising and settled his other hand against Jasper's throat again.

"I didn't say you could move," he said, pitching his voice deeper and feeling the answering skip of Jasper's heartbeat against his fingers. He leaned closer until his lips brushed Jasper's ear. "Is this what you want, slut?" he asked, finding a nipple and pinching it between his fingers.

Jasper whimpered, a flush spreading across his cheeks as he turned his head away. "No."

Vincent smirked against his neck before biting the warm flesh. "Liars get punished." He dropped his hand to the front of Jasper's pants and squeezed him through the rough fabric, and Jasper arched with a gasp and flexed his wrists. Vincent obliged and let him go, only for Jasper to stumble forward and catch himself against Vincent's chest, where he latched on to his shirt as he gasped for breath.

Vincent waited a long moment until Jasper's breathing steadied, then tipped his head up with fingers beneath his chin. His face was still flushed, and his eyes were dark, so Vincent wasn't worried that he'd crossed a line. "Well?" he asked softly. "Was that what you were looking for?"

Jasper licked his lips and blinked at Vincent a few times. "Yes, Sir." He hesitated before straightening and wrapping his arms around Vincent. "But I thought you were going to menace me?"

With a soft growl, he settled his hand on Jasper's ass. Of all the ways he could menace Jasper, the only one he could think of was the same idle fantasy he'd been entertaining since Jasper circled role-play on the list. The possibility of finally having a willing partner was almost terrifying. Without entirely meaning to, he let the words slip out. "I could menace you better as a doctor."

Jasper blinked before leaning in with a grin and stealing a quick kiss. "Are you a good doctor or an evil doctor?"

Vincent tightened his arms around Jasper. "Obviously good… at being evil."

The flush returned as Jasper stared intently at where his fingers were buried in Vincent's shirt. "So, a doctor who would ignore me saying no?"

"I could," he replied slowly. "Do you want to try that?" When Jasper nodded, Vincent stepped back and caught Jasper's hand to lead him to the playroom. He had to force his breathing to remain steady on the way down the hall. He'd never admit how often he'd imagined a similar scenario, but it was enough that he didn't need to consider how to set it up.

He flipped on the light and tugged Jasper to the corner where the exam chair was. The small chest beside it had a few medical gowns and a large white doctor coat folded neatly in a drawer. He handed one of the former to Jasper. "Strip and put this on. And you'll need a reason for going to the doctor."

Jasper shook the gown out before draping it over the chair. "Any reason?"

Vincent shrugged, biting his tongue against offering the more obvious choices to see what Jasper would come up with.

It wasn't until Jasper was slipping off his shirt that he seemed to realize buttons were missing. His face heated again as he fingered a loose thread. Vincent gave him a few seconds to offer any kind of protest and finally prompted him with a "Too much?"

Jasper shrugged with a twitch of his lips. "It was hot," he admitted softly. "I liked it."

Vincent leaned in for a quick kiss. "Noted. Do you have a scenario in mind?"

Jasper let the shirt slide off his shoulders and tossed it to the side. "Not being able to get it up?" he asked, staring at the gown as he dropped his pants, the flush spreading to his ears.

Vincent eyed the obvious semi in Jasper's boxers before turning to rummage through the various chests and cabinets around the room. He found what he was looking for in the fourth one and opened the package on his way back to Jasper, who had the gown on and was sitting on the side of the exam table, hunched forward like a patient waiting on a late doctor. He set the packaging aside and held up the two cuff restraints, one noticeably smaller than the other, held together by a short chain.

Jasper stared at it in confusion but obediently stood and pushed his boxers down when Vincent told him to. He secured the larger cuff on Jasper's thigh, then guided his cock down and to the side to fasten the smaller one around it, effectively trapping it against his leg. "Good?" he asked as he pulled the boxers back into place.

"Uh-huh," Jasper said, scooting back on the table again.

"Ready, then?" When Jasper nodded Vincent picked up the white coat and slipped it on. A clipboard with blank paper and a few pens were in another drawer, and he was impressed at how much detail Zach had put into every corner of the room.

He stood with his back to Jasper for a moment as he imagined a shady doctor with questionable morals. His last patient of the day. Most of the staff already gone or in the process of leaving. A young male patient with symptoms of erectile dysfunction.

He lifted the clipboard as if reading it as he turned and stepped closer to Jasper. "I'm Dr. Thornwell. What seems to be the issue today?" he asked, looking up and pausing as if seeing Jasper for the first time. He'd found Jasper attractive when he first came into Touch of Leather, but he'd been far more concerned with the fact someone with a new-player wristband had been sitting in his club staring at their phone instead of interacting with anyone. He gave Jasper a once-over before grabbing the stool tucked in the corner and rolling it over to sit closer.

Jasper shifted, his fingers bunched in the front of his gown. "I uh… have had some trouble getting it up."

Vincent nodded and scribbled on the paper as if writing something down. "Is it affecting your sex life?"

Jasper shrugged. "Don't really have one," he said, and Vincent resisted the urge to kiss him. He'd done role-play scenes with others on occasion, and the biggest drawback wasn't lack of ideas or enthusiasm but finding someone who could step into another character and make it feel natural and believable.

He cleared his throat and scribbled more illegible nonsense. "No girlfriend?"

“I’m gay.”

“No boyfriend?”

“No.”

Vincent nodded and crossed his legs, resting the clipboard on his knee. “So you start masturbating and nothing happens?”

“No. I can get hard, but then it kinda….” He angled his fingers down and whistled as he dropped his hand like it was dive-bombing.

“And that happens more often than not?” He made more “notes” when Jasper nodded. “When’s the last time you had an orgasm?”

Jasper murmured something under his breath.

“I didn’t catch that.”

“A couple months, maybe.”

“Well, we can run some tests. Check your testosterone levels. Though you’re young enough I doubt that’s the problem,” Vincent murmured. He glanced up, tapping the end of his pen against the clipboard. “There are some other treatments we can explore, though they’re still experimental.”

“Like what?”

“We could try various stimulants while you’re here. See if we can’t get an orgasm.”

“O-okay.”

Vincent raised an eyebrow. “You don’t seem so sure. We can wait for the test resul—”

“No, no, we can try… something.”

He nodded and stood to set the clipboard aside. A metal rack with wheels and a curtain was propped against the wall, and he rolled it over to position it beside the table. “Go ahead and lie back,” he said, waiting for Jasper to get settled before pulling out the built-in padded cuffs near the head of the table. He adjusted them down to rest near Jasper’s waist. “Put your arms through these.” Once Jasper’s wrists were secured, he rotated the attached metal bars back so Jasper’s hands were near his head instead.

Jasper squeaked when the bars locked into place with a loud click. “Are these really necessary?”

“Of course. Special stimulation,” Vincent replied, reaching for the curtain and pulling it across Jasper’s stomach so Jasper couldn’t see the lower half of his body. Then Vincent moved to the end of the bed and slipped his hands under Jasper’s gown. “Let’s get these out of the way." He ignored Jasper's yelp of protest as he tugged the boxers off and dropped them to the floor.

The novelty of the scene nearly overwhelmed him, and he had to take a moment to keep his breathing steady. He let his hands linger on Jasper's calves for a long moment before guiding his feet into the stirrups. More straps were attached to them that let him secure Jasper's ankles and thighs, and then Jasper was fully restrained.

"Um, I don't think I want to do this after all."

Vincent leaned to the side enough to glance around the curtain and met Jasper's eye. Actively saying no in a scene and proceeding anyway was new, and playing it out was always risky, but he trusted Jasper to use his actual safeword if this didn't live up to his imagination.

"Nonsense," Vincent murmured, resting his hand on Jasper's knee and slowly sliding up his thigh. "This'll be good for you. I can't possibly let you leave without you getting a proper orgasm, now can I?"

Jasper sucked in a sharp breath and licked his lower lip. "What are you gonna do to me?"

Vincent slid his hand higher with a low chuckle, dragging his fingers to a stop an inch below where Jasper's cock was strapped to his thigh. "You'll see soon enough." With that he turned to rifle through the drawers. He passed over the packs of needles, scalpels, and various medical tools until he found something he could use. An automatic cock pumping machine.

He kept himself between it and Jasper as he plugged it in and set it at the end of the exam table. Then he found lube, a latex-free glove, and a condom and rolled the stool closer, effectively hiding from Jasper's line of sight. He tugged Jasper down a bit so his ass was at the edge of the table, inched the gown higher, tucked the sides under Jasper's hips, and adjusted the stirrups to give himself a nice view.

Despite the fact he'd explored every inch of Jasper over their few months together, he still relished having his pet spread out in front of him. All that warm supple flesh, his for the taking. Resisting the urge to get his mouth on Jasper, he pulled on a glove and coated his fingers with lube. "You'll feel a bit of pressure," he said before circling his fingertips against Jasper's entrance.

Jasper responded with a quiet moan, the vinyl of the exam table squeaking with his movements.

Vincent took his time, longer than he usually did even when indulging in tormenting Jasper. Circling and nudging, pressing a fingertip inside to wiggle it before retreating and starting over. With Jasper's cock trapped against his leg, he couldn't get fully erect, and Vincent intended to keep him like that. At least for a bit.

With his other hand he stroked his thumb along Jasper's length and let out a soft hum. "I see what you mean," he said, chuckling at Jasper's indignant grumble. "Do you have toys at home?" he asked, slipping two fingers into Jasper before he could answer.

"No," he gasped. "Just a plug."

"And you can't get off while using it?" He curled his fingers and pressed against Jasper's prostate.

"Is that really important?"

"It might be. If you've already tried getting off while being filled, this could be a waste of time." He punctuated his words with a third finger and a firm thrust, humming softly in approval at Jasper's pleading groan.

"I ha-haven't."

"We'll try that, then."

"Try what?" Jasper asked, but Vincent ignored him as he pulled his fingers out and stood to push the rack with the curtain back to Jasper's shoulders for more room. The gown followed a moment later, baring Jasper's stomach and chest.

As tempted as he was to torment Jasper's nipples, he decided to leave them alone for now. Instead, he got his pants open and a condom in place.

"Wait. What are you doing?"

"Shh, relax," Vincent soothed as he gripped Jasper's hips and dragged his ass an inch off the table. "You'll feel a bit more pressure," he said and pushed inside, gritting his teeth against the intense pleasure. More intense than usual.

Jasper let out a sharp moan, his thighs straining against the bindings, and Vincent gave in to his need to get his mouth on Jasper even if it meant breaking character.

He leaned down and licked Jasper from stomach to nipple before sinking his teeth into it. Jasper's yelp only served to urge him onto the other nipple, and a few thrusts later he was coming like he was a decade younger and had little control over his body. With a silent curse he dropped his forehead to Jasper's chest to catch his breath.

He'd meant to last at least long enough to make Jasper beg, but apparently that was too much to ask for.

Jasper shifted beneath him with a breathless, "That didn't work."

Vincent huffed a laugh against Jasper's stomach and carefully pulled away. "I guess we'll have to try something else."

CHAPTER 9

FUUUUCK, THAT sounded like a threat and a promise both, and Jasper was more than ready for it. Not being able to see what Vincent was doing even though he wasn't blindfolded was a whole new level of torment. If not for the way his cock was trapped, he would have been begging for release by now. Especially with how much Vincent was into the whole doctor thing.

He almost regretted not trying something like this before, but kink had *so much* to explore that he doubted they'd ever run out of scenes. Certainly not now that he knew role-play was something Vincent enjoyed. Trying to get Vincent to admit to liking or wanting anything was frustrating on a good day, so Jasper definitely cataloged his reaction to playing a doctor. They'd have to try another setup or two while on vacation.

But first they needed to finish this one and hopefully get him off.

When Vincent cupped his balls and squeezed he groaned. "You call yourself a doctor?" he gasped with far less heat than he'd intended. "Taking advantage of your patients when you can't even get me off?"

Vincent's dark chuckle sent tingles down Jasper's arms. "I'll get you off. You won't be leaving until I do."

"I'll believe it when I see it." Though with the curtain filling most of his vision, he couldn't see much of anything and had to rely on his other senses. Like the warm pressure of Vincent's hands on his thigh and the sudden lack of restraint around his cock.

His moan of relief quickly turned to a sob of frustration when Vincent kept hold of him so he still couldn't get it up. "No," he whined, biting his lip against begging. He shouldn't beg. He was a patient. If anything he should be irritated and scathing. "What kind of quack doctor are you anyway? Fucking your own patient. I should report you to the board."

"But you won't," Vincent replied, sounding amused, the bastard.

"You don't think I will?" He stifled a gasp as something tight slipped over his cock.

"I know you won't, because I'm about to solve your little problem."

Jasper's indignation about his *so*-not-little problem died in his throat when whatever Vincent put on him began moving. Or sucking. He couldn't quite tell which and didn't care because it felt amazing. His eyes rolled back as pleasure surged through him. For a moment he was left dizzy; all his blood rushed down to his cock as it finally got the freedom it deserved.

A long groan tore out of his throat, followed by another, then a gasping whimper. If he'd thought Vincent's orgasm was quick, it was an eternity compared to how fast Jasper approached the edge. And then was left there when the amazing sensation disappeared, leaving only the tight constriction of whatever Vincent attached to him.

"No," he sobbed.

"Oh, are you close already?"

Jasper opened his mouth to tell him off, but he only managed a choked groan as Vincent pushed two fingers into him.

"No danger of drooping," Vincent continued, clinical and unaffected. Of course he was. He'd already gotten off so he could focus on tormenting Jasper as long as he wanted.

"Don't be a dick," he grumbled through his teeth.

"You want my dick?"

Yes, please. "Don't you dare," he snarled, or tried to. He hoped he didn't sound as needy as he thought he did, but even that concern became obsolete when Vincent gave a sharp tug on his hips. If not for the restraints on both his arms and legs, he was sure he would have followed his ass off the table onto the floor. A moment later the curtain was shoved aside, and Vincent leaned over him, a hand braced beside Jasper's head while the other dug a bruising mark into his ass.

Vincent's eyes were dark with a thin ring of bright hazel, and he let out a guttural moan as he pressed inside Jasper again.

"Yeah," Jasper gasped, giving up on playing the shocked patient. That wasn't Dr. Thornwell anymore. It was only Vincent, turned on and focused entirely on Jasper. He arched his body as much as he could, hating how he couldn't get any of his limbs wrapped around Vincent, and resorted to begging. "Please. Please let me come."

"Not stopping you," Vincent murmured as he fastened his lips against Jasper's neck.

His next round of pleas died off the moment Vincent began thrusting in earnest, and a few thrusts later the sucking friction returned, effectively reducing his mind to the white noise of overwhelming pleasure. Vincent's body was hot against his, his teeth leaving sharp sparks of bright color in Jasper's vision.

He sank into the bliss, trusting that Vincent's words meant he could come when he wanted. He held off as long as he could despite how close he was, though he was sure it was barely minutes before he was riding the edge. When he forced his eyes open, he was immediately transfixed by Vincent's intense gaze, hovering a breath away, and the play-by-play of his pleasure. The way his cheeks were warmed with the flush of sex, his quick breaths interspersed with soft grunts.

Vincent ducked his head as he snapped his hips in a harder thrust. A few strands of hair fell over his forehead, and Jasper desperately wanted to push them back into place. To run his fingers through Vincent's hair, curl his fingers tight, and pull him in for a kiss.

Vincent's lips twitched, not quite smile, not quite smirk. "Enjoying yourself, slut?"

Jasper swallowed a moan and somehow managed to find a bratty, "I would be if you were better at your job."

"Feisty," Vincent purred, pressing his face against Jasper's neck, hot breaths followed by a wet swipe of tongue, and then Vincent shuddered with a low, sweet moan of release.

Jasper's sudden disappointment that he couldn't feel Vincent coming inside him didn't last long before he tipped over the edge himself.

Vincent held still for a moment as they caught their breaths, and Jasper was sure he didn't imagine the light press of a kiss against his shoulder before Vincent pulled away. He released Jasper's arms and legs, but Jasper made no effort to get up, remaining in a blissed-out, boneless sprawl as he watched Vincent dispose of the condoms and remove some sort of pump from Jasper, then snag a small towel to wipe them both down. He tossed everything into a small pile before turning to Jasper and helping him sit up.

Jasper tipped his head back and was rewarded with a slow kiss. He latched on to Vincent's sleeves with a pleased moan.

"Good?"

Jasper smiled. "Great. Ready for a nap." Vincent snorted and helped him upstairs where he collapsed onto the bed and stretched out. "Nap with me," he said, holding an arm out, beyond pleased when Vincent settled in next to him. Jasper snuggled in and tucked his head under Vincent's chin. "So, I was thinking," he said, tipping his head back when Vincent chuckled. "What?"

"I'll have to work harder to make sure you can't think after a scene."

"Mm, good luck." He shifted closer and wiggled a leg between Vincent's with a happy sigh, closing his eyes when Vincent's fingers worked through his hair. "I was thinking… you could stop using condoms." He smirked when Vincent's fingers tightened in his hair. He nuzzled Vincent's throat before lightly biting when he didn't respond.

"What changed your mind?"

Jasper shivered at the rough edge in Vincent's voice and pressed his face into Vincent's shoulder. As if that would make answering any easier. "When you came, I wanted to know what it felt like," he murmured.

"And you still want to know?"

Jasper shrugged then nodded, keeping his face hidden, but Vincent didn't let him hide long before tugging his head back. The kiss was slow and thorough and almost enough to get him going again, if he hadn't just had one of the best orgasms of his life. He even managed to get his fingers tangled in Vincent's hair without his arms being pinned.

When Vincent finally pulled back, Jasper's lips were tingling. "You like the idea that much?" he asked, only a little breathless.

Vincent studied him a moment, brushing a thumb back and forth against his jawline. "With you, yes," he finally answered.

Jasper's chest constricted. It was a far cry from a declaration of love, but somehow it felt like more. He curled his fingers tighter in Vincent's hair and pulled, and Vincent followed easily. He gave up on his plan of taking a nap. Making out with Vincent was far more fun.

CHAPTER 10

TUESDAY MORNING Jasper woke early enough to slip out of bed and make breakfast. He usually resorted to scrambled eggs and toast. Bacon if he was feeling confident. Pancakes if he had the patience. But today he wanted to try his hand at waffles. He was sure they had to be easier than pancakes, especially when the waffle iron meant they wouldn't be misshapen. Except the first one he made was not only deformed but nearly charred, and he spent ten minutes on his phone finding a recipe with easy instructions.

It took three more attempts before he made one that looked edible, and by then he realized he'd made far too much batter and had to decide whether to use it all, toss it, or save it for later. In the end he used most of it trying to make four crispy golden waffles like Vincent could make. Once he had those, he scrambled some eggs, topped them with cheese, and filled two plates. He found a serving tray to pile it all onto with two large mugs of coffee, and then he headed upstairs.

Vincent was still passed out, so he set the tray on a nightstand and crawled back into bed, where he proceeded to latch on to Vincent and nuzzle, kiss, and bite his shoulder until he woke up. With an incoherent grumble, Vincent rolled over, pinned Jasper beneath him, and buried his face in his hair. "Who disturbs my slumber?"

Jasper snickered and slid his hands down to grope Vincent's ass. "It is I, Jasper. Your humble subby slut."

Vincent pulled away with a sleep-rough laugh. "You got two of three right anyway," he murmured.

"Hey!"

Vincent smirked as he sat up and reached for a cup of coffee. He took a sip and sank against the headboard, closing his eyes with a soft hum.

"Don't go back to sleep," Jasper grumbled, reaching over Vincent for the tray and settling it over his lap before picking up a plate.

"Why not?"

"'Cause we have things to do."

"And by things, do you mean you?"

"Duh."

When Vincent shook his head, Jasper grinned and shoved a large bite of waffle into his mouth. They ate in silence until Jasper couldn't hold back anymore and propped his shoulder against Vincent's. "Sooo, is it only playing as an evil doctor you're interested in, or are there other things too?"

Vincent paused with his cup pressed against his lip, clearing his throat and taking a sip before answering. "Role-play is one of the things I enjoy most."

"Really?" he asked in surprise. "But you're always…." He flicked his fingers as he sought the right word.

"An uptight dick?" Vincent asked dryly.

Jasper elbowed him. Only he could call Vincent a dick. "Calm and collected." He shoveled the last of his eggs into his mouth, set the tray with dishes aside, then crawled into Vincent's lap to straddle his thighs. He hooked his fingers in Vincent's T-shirt. "So what else do you like to role-play?"

"Anything we can come up with." Vincent drained the rest of his coffee and leaned over to set it on the nightstand. When he turned his attention back to Jasper, he settled both hands on Jasper's hips and slid his fingers under the hem of his shirt. "Pirate and captive. Prostitute and priest. Rival mafia bosses."

Jasper's eyebrows twitched higher with each suggestion, which somehow got progressively more outlandish, but when Vincent mentioned royalty and a knight, he couldn't stop the impulse to clamp a hand over Vincent's mouth to stop him. "Like a king or… a prince?"

Vincent smiled against his palm. "Do you want to be a prince?" he asked, his words muffled.

Heat crept up Jasper's neck at the suggestion, briefly imagining Vincent sprawled out beneath him before realizing a prince could just as easily be the one on the bottom. He licked his lips and slowly removed his hand from Vincent's mouth. "Do you want to be my…." Not a knight or a guard. That sounded typical and boring. "Advisor?"

"And what would I be advising you on?"

Jasper pressed his lips together and barely managed to keep from saying *sex, obviously*. "How to be a good ruler."

"Like making sure you don't disappear every time the king mentions marriage?"

He tipped his head back with a wrinkle of his nose. “He shouldn’t keep trying to marry me off to snobby princesses.”

“A snobby prince is more to your liking, then?”

“Or a scruffy, pain-in-my-ass advisor.”

“Scruffy,” Vincent repeated, narrowing his eyes.

Jasper lifted his hands to scritch his knuckles against the two-days-worth of stubble on Vincent’s jaw. “Sexy scruffy.” He trailed his fingers down Vincent’s throat and chest. “You’re more my type. Don’t you want to advise me on how to please my future spouse?” he asked, fluttering his lashes with a small pout. “Am I not to your liking?” A thrill shivered down Jasper’s spine when Vincent’s fingers tightened on his hips.

Vincent leaned forward and dragged the tip of his nose against Jasper’s cheek before whispering in his ear. “You want me to teach you how to properly fuck your partner?”

Jasper went light-headed between the heat rushing to his face and the blood rushing to his cock. A soft strangled moan escaped him at the thought of being inside Vincent. His breath left him with a shuddery, “What?”

“Are you worried you won’t please them, Your Highness?” Vincent purred before tracing his tongue around the shell of Jasper’s ear.

He swallowed hard and twisted his fingers in Vincent’s shirt to keep himself grounded. No way was Vincent really offering to let Jasper top. Was he? “Are you serious?” he asked softly, staring at Vincent when he pulled back. “You’d really let me…?”

Vincent raised an eyebrow. “I’m not against it. Are you?”

“I—That’s not—You can’t—” He snapped his mouth shut when Vincent pressed a thumb to his lips.

“You think a sub can’t penetrate his Dom,” he said, and Jasper nodded and sagged in relief at not having to find the words. “You think because I’m your Dom I can’t enjoy being taken as much as you do?”

“Do you?” Vincent had never mentioned or given any indication he wanted that.

“With the right conditions. And the right partner,” Vincent murmured.

Jasper’s heart skipped before pounding in his chest. Vincent thought he was the right partner. Vincent thought he was the right partner? “I’ve never….”

Vincent didn’t look surprised as he brushed his thumb back and forth against Jasper’s lips. “Do you know why I like role-play?” he asked, waiting for Jasper to shake his head before continuing. "Kink lets you explore physical or mental fantasies, but role-play lets you experience different lives."

Jasper's lips twitched, and he lightly bit Vincent's thumb on its next swipe. "Like a corrupt doctor who likes to abuse his patients."

"Or a dedicated, loyal advisor who'd give everything to his prince. Even his own body."

Jasper swayed closer, his fingers splayed against Vincent's stomach as butterflies tried to burst out of his own. "What if the prince is really bad at sex?"

"He won't be," Vincent said, sliding a hand into Jasper's hair and curling into a loose grip.

"How do you know?"

"Because a good advisor won't let him be."

Jasper tipped his head back with a soft gasp when Vincent tugged, heat already pooling in his gut before Vincent's lips and his scruff left a tingling path down Jasper's neck. "Are you a good advisor?" Jasper asked.

"Only the best." Vincent lightly dragged his teeth against Jasper's shoulder before replacing them with a warm kiss. "Should I prove it, Your Highness?"

"By letting me fuck you?"

Vincent *tsk*ed and flexed his fingers tighter in Jasper's hair. "By guiding you in how to pleasure me."

Oh. That sounded less stressful. If Vincent was still in control, Jasper had less of a chance to fuck everything up. "Okay," he whispered. "What do I do?"

Vincent pulled back and settled against the headboard with an approving hum. "You can start by removing my clothes."

Surely he'd heard that wrong. He'd never seen Vincent fully and completely naked before. He knew what Vincent's scars looked like and felt like, but not an undressed Vincent. He slipped his hands under Vincent's shirt and caressed his sides and stomach. "All of them?"

"Mm-hmm." He caught Jasper's wrist when he pushed Vincent's shirt up. "Slow."

Jasper gave a jerky nod and stared at his hands as he inched Vincent's shirt up his stomach. When the edge of the burn scars came into view, he paused and glanced up to make sure Vincent was really okay with this.

"I'm sure," Vincent said softly, resting his hands on Jasper's thighs.

He caught his lower lip between his teeth and continued pushing the shirt up. As more of the scars were revealed, he dragged his thumbs against them. Burn scars were always gnarly, but Jasper found them fascinating rather than repulsive. Even a decade old, he could tell how severe the burns had been. Especially after he'd spent two days researching burn injuries in all the medical texts he could find in the college library. He'd initially started researching online, but he wanted the validity of published and peer-reviewed information.

When he finally got the shirt to Vincent's shoulders, Vincent lifted his arms so Jasper could pull it over his head and toss it aside. Then he had the luxury of Vincent half naked beneath him, and he couldn't resist exploring with his fingertips. The pale flesh and sparse scattering of dark curls across his chest. The angry red spiderweb of old scars across his torso and the jagged white one down his right arm. He spread his palm across the center of the damage and pushed past the dark flare of doubt in his gut.

Other lives, Vincent had said. What was the point in pretending to be someone or something else if they couldn't create a different story for something like this?

"Is this from when you saved my life?" he asked softly, glancing up at Vincent's sharp inhale. "From the fire that nearly killed me."

Vincent's throat worked as he swallowed, his fingers twitching against Jasper's hips before he finally nodded.

Emboldened and not about to miss the opportunity to prove to Vincent his scars weren't something to be ashamed of, Jasper slowly traced across the entire spread of scar tissue. "You nearly died because of me."

"So long as you lived, it would have been worth it."

"Don't say that," Jasper hissed. Even if this wasn't real, the thought of Vincent dying made it hard to breathe. Even worse if Vincent died because of him. "You're not allowed to die."

Vincent's lips twitched, but his voice was grave when he answered. "Yes, Your Highness."

"And don't call me highness," he grumbled, dropping his hands to Vincent's sleep pants and tugging. "Not here."

"What should I call you, then?" Vincent planted his hands against the mattress and lifted his hips to let Jasper finish undressing him.

"You could use my name."

"Prince Jasper."

"No, just my name."

"I could never be so presumptuous."

Jasper shot him an exasperated look from beneath his lashes and tossed Vincent's pants aside, his socks following. "Don't be difficult."

"Apologies, my liege."

He snorted as he settled between Vincent's legs, refusing to be intimidated. At least until Vincent picked up the bottle of lube and handed it over. Jasper's face was so hot it was a wonder his hair didn't catch fire. He popped the lube's top and squirted too much onto his fingers; then he froze as reality caught up to them and he realized he was actually about to top Vincent. His Dom. His advisor. As a sub and a prince.

The warmth of Vincent's fingers around his wrist drew him back to the moment. "Yooou should lie down," he said, hoping he sounded more confident than he felt.

"As you wish, my liege." Vincent nudged Jasper back with a knee, then stretched out on the bed, and that was somehow even more intimidating. Especially when Vincent propped a knee up to give Jasper better access. "One finger," he murmured.

A strangled groan escaped Jasper as he stared at Vincent's groin, pushing through the excitement and worry churning in his gut. He gripped Vincent's knee for balance and to keep himself from fleeing down the stairs before pressing the finger of his other hand against Vincent's entrance, circling his finger a dozen or more times as he gathered the courage and audacity he needed to finally push the tip in.

Vincent blew out a slow breath and curled his fingers around Jasper's wrist again.

When Jasper risked glancing up, Vincent's head was tipped back and his eyes were closed. Was that how he looked when Vincent was tormenting him? Relaxed and wanton. Trusting. The fact Vincent trusted him this much was like a punch to the throat. He couldn't fuck this up. "Good?"

"Good," Vincent rasped. "Been a while."

"How long?" Jasper demanded, not liking the thought of someone else seeing this side of Vincent. Which was ridiculous. Vincent was older than him, far more experienced, and owned a kink club. Even as an advisor, he'd have a life outside of being a pain in a prince's ass.

Vincent cracked his eyes open and focused on Jasper with a knowing expression. "Long before I met you, my liege."

Jasper wrinkled his nose. "Liege makes me sound like an old man."

Vincent made a strangled sound somewhere between a laugh and a groan. "We can't have that, now can we, my prince."

"Oh," he squeaked, the sudden shiver of tingles taking him by surprise. That was almost as good as Vincent calling him a slut in that rough, deep voice he liked to use. "I like that," he whispered and carefully pressed a second finger in. He nearly combusted on the spot when Vincent tipped his head back and arched with a soft gasp. "Fuck, you're hot," he breathed, leaning down to drag his tongue along the scars. He was rewarded by Vincent shuddering beneath him and clenching tight around his fingers. He closed his eyes with a low moan and tried not to imagine that sensation around his aching cock, or he'd lose it then and there.

How did Vincent manage to mercilessly torment him so easily? All Jasper wanted was to bury himself inside Vincent and take his pleasure until they were both exhausted. Somehow he found the strength to hold himself back. He couldn't rush this. Didn't want to rush this, despite his dick urging him on.

He kissed his way up Vincent's scars to his neck, releasing a shuddering breath against warm skin. "Can I mark you?" he asked softly.

Vincent buried his fingers in Jasper's hair, and his voice was rough when he answered, "Yeah."

Jasper adjusted his hand to press his fingers in deeper as he sought out Vincent's prostate, then focused on scraping his teeth against Vincent's neck and carefully biting hard enough to leave a mark. Then he did it again and again, flexing his wrist and fingers until he finally found the spot he was looking for. Vincent let out a throaty groan, and that—*that* explained everything.

Jasper told his dick to shut the fuck up and wiggled his fingertips to massage Vincent's prostate. He pressed wet kisses down Vincent's neck and throat as he cataloged his moans. What made it higher or lower, or what caused the deep groan that rumbled in his chest. His favorite was the high breathy one that sparked desire in his own gut.

By the time he'd worked three fingers in, he could taste the clean sweat on Vincent's skin, and his dark hair was damp and sticking to his temples. *Gorgeous*, Jasper thought and barely kept the word from escaping his mouth. It was somehow equally hot and endearing and embarrassing to see Vincent like this. Lost in pleasure. Then guilt settled over him for not giving Vincent this release earlier.

Vincent was always calm and collected, focused on making sure Jasper enjoyed every scene. Sure, Vincent took his pleasure too, but never like this. When was the last time Vincent was able to lie back and be taken care of? Since his bitch of an ex? Before?

"I think you've mastered step one," Vincent murmured, clearly ready to move on.

Jasper was almost content to keep tormenting him, to make Vincent come apart on his fingers, but who knew when he'd have the chance for this again? "Condom?" he asked, propping himself up with his free hand and nudging Vincent's prostate a few more times before sliding his fingers out.

Vincent groaned and reached for the drawer, blindly rummaging until he snagged a condom and held it up. He held on to it when Jasper tried to take it, and Jasper glanced up to meet Vincent's intense hazel stare. "You don't have to use it."

"You're sure?"

"If you're sure you want to stop using them, yes," he said and let go of the packet.

Jasper swallowed hard, turning the condom over between his fingers. He'd seen the test results, which was more reassurance than anyone else had ever given him. What more could he possibly need? He tossed the condom aside and surged forward to seal their lips together. He meant to keep it short and sweet, but Vincent caught him with both hands in his hair, curled his fingers tight, and kept him in place while Vincent kissed him senseless. Enough that Jasper nearly forgot he was supposed to be a prince.

He was dazed when it finally ended and he dragged his tongue along his lower lip until his brain caught up again. "So I just… put it in?"

"Slowly and with lube."

Jasper rested his forehead against Vincent's cheek with a long exhale. He could do this. Except once he'd covered his dick in lube and lined up, the angle was too awkward, and he couldn't bring himself to put Vincent's leg over his shoulder.

Thankfully Vincent took pity on him and handed over a pillow, which Jasper shoved under Vincent's hips. Then he settled his hands on Vincent's thighs and pressed inside him.

"Oh. Oh gods. Oh fuck." The tight heat gripping him was better than he'd ever imagined. Better than whatever toy Vincent had used on him the day before. Better than Vincent sucking him off around a condom. His hips twitched forward, and it took every ounce of willpower not to bury himself with one quick thrust. Watching Vincent didn't curb that desire either. His head thrown back, one hand fisted in the sheets, the other gripping Jasper's wrist.

Jasper's fingers dug bruises into Vincent's thighs, and his lungs nearly popped from holding his breath as he steadily inched inside until he was fully seated. He slumped forward and dropped his forehead to Vincent's chest as he gasped for air. "Gods, you feel so good."

"So do you." Vincent exhaled a groan and slid his hand to the back of Jasper's neck. "You can move."

"Nuh-uh." It was a miracle he hadn't come already from the sheer ecstasy of being inside Vincent. "Can't yet."

Vincent chuckled and flexed his fingers in Jasper's hair. "Enjoying yourself, my prince?"

"*Nnngh.*" Jasper turned his head enough to nip at Vincent's wrist. "A lot." He slid his palms up Vincent's sides and across his chest, relishing having his hands free during sex for once and being able to touch. "A lot a lot," he murmured, stretching out over Vincent and giving an experimental thrust of his hips. "Fuuuuck," he groaned. How could Vincent make every scene last for what seemed like hours when it felt this good?

Vincent made that breathy moan again when he moved his hips faster, and Jasper zeroed in on that. He braced his hands on either side of Vincent and watched his face, using his reactions as a guide until he earned one of those amazing sounds with nearly every thrust.

"Harder, my prince," Vincent ordered.

Jasper gasped at the intense pleasure that crashed through him. His hips stuttered despite his best efforts to hold back his orgasm, and suddenly his movements became much slicker. The guilt and embarrassment for coming too soon was short-lived. He'd barely caught his breath before he was ready for round two. That had never happened before, but neither had he ever been balls deep inside someone before.

Even as the bliss of release wore off, he was half hard again, but with post-nut clarity he was able to focus far more of his attention on Vincent.

He settled into moving his hips at an excruciatingly slow pace and used both hands to explore every inch of Vincent's chest before resting on his stomach. "Well?" he rasped. "Shouldn't you be advising me?"

Vincent exhaled a laugh and cracked his eyes open. "You could move faster."

Jasper grinned. "I could," he said. It probably wasn't his best idea to give Vincent a taste of his own medicine, but he couldn't resist. Besides, he hadn't hated any punishment yet, so he wasn't likely to regret it. Much. So he kept his pace slow as his body ramped up again and inched his fingers down to caress Vincent's hips and thighs.

"Never thought I'd see you like this," he murmured and promptly shut his mouth when he remembered he was a prince and not a sub. Except a prince wouldn't need to watch his tongue. Not with his advisor. "Always so uptight. Always have something to correct me on." He leaned over Vincent and braced his hands on either side of him as he gave a hard thrust, wicked glee sparking in his chest when Vincent tipped his head back with a sharp groan. Or was it a whine?

"Nothing to say now? Is my cock that good?" he taunted, which was apparently Vincent's limit of Jasper's antics.

With a twist of his lower body Vincent had Jasper flat on his back with his hands pinned beside his head.

For a moment Jasper could only stare, somehow even more turned on as Vincent began moving. He let out a startled "Oh" that ended on a moan. Was that what it looked and felt like to have someone riding him? He'd tried resisting the same position himself. Somehow it was too exposed, which made absolutely no sense considering all the ways Vincent restrained him. But staring up at Vincent as he rode Jasper was one of the hottest things he'd seen yet. No wonder Vincent had wanted Jasper to ride him like this before, albeit with his hands restrained behind his back.

Vincent closed the distance between them to murmur against Jasper's lips. "My dear prince is as infuriating as ever."

"You like when I—" He lost his train of thought when it exploded from whatever trick Vincent did with his hips. Vincent's smug chuckle only fanned the flames until Jasper was lost in an inferno with no desire to escape. "Fuck," he breathed, sealing his lips to Vincent's. He twisted his wrists free without much effort and buried one hand in Vincent's hair to keep him close as he wrapped the other around Vincent's cock.

Vincent grunted and bucked into Jasper's hand, his eyes squeezed shut and his breaths ragged against Jasper's lips.

That wouldn't do at all, though the words to fix it stuck in Jasper's throat. Taunting Vincent was one thing, but ordering him to do something, even in a scene like this—wasn't that crossing a line? Fuck it. He swallowed hard and tightened his fingers in Vincent's hair. "Eyes on me."

Vincent tilted his head and cracked his eyes open, dark rings of hazel hovering an inch away from Jasper's own.

The "Good boy" slipped out before Jasper could even think of biting it back. The surprise that flickered across Vincent's face was at least better than anger or annoyance, but an apology still hovered on his tongue until the surprise vanished beneath pleasure as Vincent's orgasm hit. Jasper gasped as Vincent tightened around him, gritting his teeth against giving in to his own orgasm and pumping his hand over Vincent as he pulsed and came on Jasper's stomach.

A few breaths later Vincent focused on him and kept moving until Jasper gave up any hope of holding back and came a second time.

He slumped with a breathless laugh and turned his head to nuzzle Vincent's wrist where it was still planted next to the pillow. "That was.... Wow."

Vincent hummed and lifted off Jasper, but when he leaned to the side as if to climb off the bed Jasper stopped him with a hand on his hip to nudge him the other way.

"I'll get it," he said, quickly wiggling off the bed while trying not to leave a mess everywhere. His body was overenergized as he cleaned himself up in the bathroom before taking a warm cloth back to Vincent, who was stretched out on his back with an arm over his eyes. Heat crept up his neck as he settled on the bed, but Vincent always made a point to clean them up after a scene, so he powered through the embarrassment. He tossed the cloth aside when he was done and curled up against Vincent, his arm still covering half his face.

"Was... that okay?"

"You were amazing," Vincent said without moving.

Jasper tried not to overthink it, failed, and didn't try again. "Are *you* okay?"

Vincent curled his fingers into a fist before releasing it with a slow breath. "Yes."

Jasper propped his chin on Vincent's chest. "Was it the good boy?" he asked, somehow managing to keep his voice light despite the sense that he'd done something wrong.

That was finally enough for Vincent to shift his wrist aside to give Jasper a dry look. Even suspecting that had been a step too far didn't prepare him for Vincent's "Yes. I wasn't expecting that."

"Bad?"

"No." Vincent lifted his other hand to Jasper's hair and buried his fingers in it with a soft sigh. "Just unexpected."

Jasper leaned into the touch with a frown. "Why? You are a good boy." He grinned at Vincent's unamused stare and turned his head to bite his wrist. "The bestest boy."

"Am I a dog now?"

"Nah. You're still the decrepit owner of a mangy cat," he said and rolled off the bed when Vincent laughed. He found his boxers to pull on and headed to the kitchen. They'd need to hydrate before another round… or whatever Vincent had planned for the rest of the day.

Chapter 11

Christ, he was sore. At least it wasn't as bad as Vincent remembered, but years with only the occasional slender plug to scratch that particular itch was no preparation for the real thing. Even a hot shower hadn't offered more than superficial relief, but that was fine.

The ache was worth Jasper discovering something new. Seeing how he stepped into a role as easily and completely as everything else they'd tried, he was surprised by the way Jasper mimicked his style, but maybe he shouldn't have been. Vincent was the only one Jasper had played with or subbed for, so it made sense he'd use what he'd learned, but Vincent still hadn't expected to have his own methods turned on him.

He settled on the sofa and stretched his legs out. He found the remote to turn on the TV and flipped through the channels to find a movie while his phone booted up for his nightly missed call check. Not that he expected to hear from anyone, at least not about anything important, but he couldn't quite bring himself to ignore his phone for two full weeks.

When Jasper finished with the dishes and joined him, he straddled Vincent's lap and leaned in for a kiss. The lack of hesitation or second-guessing was new and a turn-on, and Vincent tossed the remote aside in favor of making out with his sub. They'd barely gotten started when his phone chimed with a text, which he ignored. A few minutes later it rang, and Vincent broke the kiss with an annoyed huff to answer it. "Yes?"

"Oh, am I interrupting something?" Zach asked with a snicker.

"Yes."

"Too bad. I need an answer to my text."

Vincent let out a slow breath for patience and ignored Jasper's amused stare as he pulled up his texts.

Lunch tomorrow y/y?

"Funny, it sounds like we don't have a choice," Vincent said.

"You don't," Zach replied with a grin evident in his voice. "But I need to know what to make. My spaghetti isn't nearly as good as yours. Your boy have any allergies?"

"He doesn't like olives."

He barely heard Zach's "Good God, there's two of them now," since he was completely distracted by Jasper's surprised smile. As if he thought Vincent wouldn't remember. Then he was distracted by Jasper's lips against his neck and the fingers worming their way under his shirt.

Zach cleared his throat. "Are you even listening?"

"No."

"Man, you've got it bad." He was well aware of that, but hearing Zach point it out wasn't entirely comforting. "I asked if chicken parm would work. I'll even make my super special potatoes."

"Putting butter and roasted garlic on a pack of instant potatoes doesn't make them special," Vincent replied dryly.

Jasper snorted and buried his face against Vincent's neck to muffle his laugh.

"Rude. It'll be ready by one, so be here before then. Clothing optional."

"Absolutely not," Vincent muttered. "Clothing required."

"Take all the fun out of everything, why don't you?"

"Bye."

Vincent hung up on Zach's second "Rude!" and dropped the phone to the floor. Any further interruptions would have to wait.

VINCENT STILL had an ache in his back come morning, but it wasn't entirely unpleasant. After a quick breakfast he sent Jasper to the playroom to pick out some Shibari ropes while he flipped through some images on his phone. Most were simple loops with knots, but he wanted something a bit more intricate. He'd watched some videos in his spare time over the past weeks to refresh himself in the hopes of Aston and Jasper agreeing to a photo shoot.

Jasper returned with a few loops of rope in black and dark plum.

Vincent turned his phone off and tossed it aside to take the rope and set it on his other side. Jasper was dressed in only a pair of boxers, and he indulged in all the bare flesh available to him.

Jasper straddled his lap with happy sounds and ran his fingers through Vincent's hair. "Anything I need to know about your friends?"

"Zach can be pretty tactile, especially if he takes a liking to you. Ash doesn't speak much." Vincent trailed his fingers down Jasper's thighs. "If they make you uncomfortable and you want to leave just say so."

Jasper pulled back enough to eye him with a frown. "Are you worried I won't like them?"

Vincent opened his mouth to answer, but he realized he really wasn't. Zach and Ash had both despised Adam even before Vincent fell into a toxic relationship with him. Zach made no secret of hating him but was at least civilly polite to him. Adam complained so much after the single time Zach and Ash visited that Vincent fell out of touch with them.

"No," he finally said. If he were honest, he was more terrified of how well Jasper and Zach might get along. They were both brats, but Zach had a devious streak wide enough to rival the Grand Canyon. "I think you'll get along fine."

He picked up one of the lengths of black rope and set to work. He was still out of practice enough that some of the diamonds were uneven, but they had enough time that he redid them until he was satisfied. Jasper was as pliable as ever, easily moving where Vincent directed or maneuvered him. By the time he used all the black and reached for the purple, Jasper's breathing had deepened, his expression was calm, and he was certainly enjoying himself if the growing situation in his boxers was any indication.

When he'd finished with Jasper's torso it was covered in a pattern of small diamonds. His arms had a line of rope down the outsides with four loops spaced out from biceps to wrists. He wound the extra length around the lines, then settled his hands on Jasper's legs to admire his work.

"Should we add your fox ears?" he asked, smirking when Jasper came out of his stupor enough to shoot him an annoyed glare. "I'll take that as a no." He landed a light swat against Jasper's ass and toppled him to the sofa, then headed upstairs to rummage through Jasper's clothes. He picked out a pair of jeans and a deep red button-up shirt that made Jasper's blue eyes appear brighter.

Jasper raised an eyebrow when Vincent handed them over, but he pulled them on, his lips twitching when Vincent undid the top few buttons and tugged the collar farther apart so the Shibari was visible. "Are you trying to make me look good?"

"Problem?"

"Depends. You're not trying to set up an orgy or something, are you?"

Vincent paused and slowly hooked a finger through one of the diamonds below Jasper's throat, the possessive need to keep Jasper all to himself warring with the voyeur inside him who wouldn't mind sharing with someone he trusted. "Is that something you're interested in?"

Jasper blinked, a flush spreading across his cheeks. "Not really."

He didn't comment on the uncertain tone. Even if Jasper was interested, it wouldn't happen today. He gave a light tug on the rope, humming softly when Jasper rocked onto the balls of his feet, his pupils dilating. "Go fix your hair," he said and let go to get dressed himself. As much as he preferred a suit, he didn't need to give Zach even more ammo to add to his ample supply.

He pulled on black jeans and a heather gray graphic tee with "The Rabbit of Caerbannog is my Spirit Animal" scrawled across it in fancy black script. It earned an amused eye-roll from Jasper, and he couldn't resist hooking a finger in the Shibari to pull him closer, which only amused him more.

"You like that entirely too much, Sir."

Vincent huffed softly and didn't bother to point out that Jasper likely enjoyed it more. "A leash would be better." He slipped his fingers down to tweak a nipple before heading for the door. They'd be a little early, but at least with others around, he'd be slightly less tempted to torment his pet.

Chapter 12

JASPER TUGGED at the hem of his shirt as he followed Vincent up the stairs to a large cabin, the slight rough-soft texture of the Shibari rope rasping against his skin with every breath. The door swung open before Vincent even knocked, and a short, lanky man with black hair looked them over with a critical eye.

"Well, well, aren't you a catch," he said with a grin. "Gorgeous. The rope's pretty too." He reached out and hooked an arm around Jasper's before he could respond and tugged him inside. "I'm Zach, by the way."

Jasper glanced at Vincent in bewilderment, but Vincent merely shook his head and shut the door behind them.

"I asked you not to scar him."

Zach ignored that as he called out, "Aaash. Come meet the sweet little thing Master Vincent finally found."

Jasper helplessly followed Zach to the combined dining room and kitchen where a short blond man was chopping vegetables at the counter. When he turned Jasper got a good view of the black leather collar around his throat. He wasn't sure why, but he'd instinctively marked Zach as the sub in the relationship, but the collar suggested otherwise. He managed a weak "Hi" when Zach finally stopped moving.

Ash glanced over with a nod and quiet greeting. "Nice to meet you," he said with a British accent that took Jasper by surprise.

Zach patted Jasper's arm as Ash returned his attention to chopping. "Sexy accent, yeah? Too bad he doesn't talk much," he said with fond exasperation. He turned them to the living room and pulled Jasper down to sit beside him on the sofa.

Jasper glanced back at the kitchen, where Vincent was quietly talking with Ash, until Zach drew his attention back with a poke to his cheek.

"So how long have you been together?" Zach asked, eyeing Jasper with a sly grin.

"A few months. Almost five."

His grin widened. "Ohhh. Second contract, then." He patted Jasper's arm again. "And he's treating you well?"

Jasper reflexively tensed. "Yes," he said and wondered if he was going to have to fight Zach for speaking badly of Vincent, but he only laughed.

"Master Vincent is one of the best men I know. You're lucky you caught his eye."

The fight went out of him, and Jasper slumped against the sofa. Maybe he'd only been expecting the worst because the people he lived with and knew Vincent better than he did disapproved of their relationship. Matt openly hated Vincent, and Amber and the others avoided talking about him as if they were allergic to his name. It was nice to finally meet someone who actually liked him. "How do you know him?"

"Oxford." Zach chuckled when Jasper's eyebrows shot up. "We both went for a business degree. His grandmother hates my guts since a lowly American could never live up to her standards," he said with a dismissive wave of his hand. He leaned in with a conspiratorial whisper. "You should hear his British accent."

"I heard that," Vincent said from the entrance of the room.

Jasper turned towards him with wide eyes. "You've been denying me the chance to hear your accent, Sir?"

Vincent scoffed as Zach snickered. "Absolutely not," he said, moving to sit on the love seat.

Jasper started to get up to join him, but Zach still had an arm looped around his, and it was kinda nice being around others who weren't being assholes. He resorted to pouting instead. "Is it a bad accent? Like Keanu Reeves' Dracula bad?"

Zach hummed and tapped a finger against his chin in exaggerated consideration. "I don't know… Is it that bad?"

Vincent narrowed his eyes, which only made Jasper more curious and determined to hear it.

"Pleaaase, Master Vincent?" he tried, which earned a startled look from Vincent while Zach failed to stifle his laughter.

Vincent scowled at them both before sighing. "What do you want me to say?"

Zach leaned in to whisper in Jasper's ear, and he dutifully repeated, "Bottle of water?"

Vincent glowered at Zach. "No."

"Aww, you're no fun," Zach huffed.

"Tell me you're going to tie me up and spank me."

Zach whistled.

Vincent turned a heated gaze on Jasper. When he spoke his voice was deeper and his words were softened by longer vowels. "I'm going to string you up, spank you till you scream, and take my time tormenting you."

Jasper's pants were suddenly a bit too tight. "That was really hot, Sir."

Zach nodded. "Definitely going to help you get laid tonight."

"I do not need help getting laid," Vincent replied, still with an accent, and Jasper grinned.

"No, but if you talk to me like that in a scene, I might not be able to control myself."

"You two are so disgusting," Zach cooed. "I like him," he said to Vincent. "Much better than fuckface."

Jasper couldn't control his reflexive sneer. "You mean douche canoe?"

"Oh, you've met him."

"Unfortunately." And he hoped it was the only time since he still wanted to punch the bastard in the face.

Zach rubbed Jasper's arm. "Don't worry. You're prettier."

"Don't encourage him."

"Yes, encourage me," Jasper said, leaning into Zach with a forlorn sigh. "Master Vincent is so mean to me."

Zach gasped and wrapped his arms tight around Jasper as he glared at Vincent. "How dare he torment such a sweet soul."

Vincent tipped his head back. "I knew I would regret this. Just so you know, I only came so I could borrow Ash for the photo shoot."

"And here I thought you were going to ask for new furniture."

"I might have before you turned my sub against me."

Zach made a shooing motion at Vincent. "Oh, go bother Ash with your photo ideas and spare us your foul mood."

Vincent eyed them both with suspicion but finally stood and went back to the kitchen.

Jasper watched him go, though he wasn't nearly as apprehensive about being left alone as he was a few minutes ago. Zach poked his cheek, and he turned his head. "What?"

"Ohhh, nothing. Just glad to see he found someone who makes him happy."

He tried not to let that go to his head. "How do you know?"

Zach snorted and flicked his fingers. "'Cause I've seen him miserable. Even with fuckface he was miserable, but in a different way." He sighed and propped their shoulders together. "Please tell me you're a brat. He needs a proper brat in his life."

Jasper couldn't stop his grin, and Zach cackled.

"I knew it," he said, lifting his hand for a fist bump. "So, here's what you wanna do…."

Chapter 13

Jasper wasn't sure if he should be more amazed or terrified of Zach. It was clear he had years more experience than Jasper and was knowledgeable about kink, especially about being a brat, which wasn't surprising. He didn't know Doms could be brats, but now that he thought about it, Vincent being a dick was basically brat behavior. Maybe that was why they got along so well.

Well enough that he was hesitant to actually try any of Zach's many, many suggestions, though the insider information and confirmation that role-play was one of Vincent's biggest kinks was appreciated. Most of Zach's ideas sounded like deliberately being a general nuisance until Vincent punished him, and Jasper wasn't quite up to pushing his luck that far.

The idea of teasing him, though….

He polished off the last bite of his blueberry cheesecake, then slumped against Vincent's side as he fought off a food coma with a soft moan. "I ate too much."

Zach chuckled and sipped his coffee. "Glad you liked it." He tilted his head as he glanced at Ash. "Did you decide?" When Ash nodded, Zach turned back to Jasper. "If you want to see some of his work, his studio is downstairs."

Jasper eyed Zach and Vincent and took the hint. "Sure," he said and followed Ash to a set of stairs leading to a basement. The room was significantly cooler than upstairs, but the countless photos lining the walls distracted him from any discomfort.

Most were bodies in various states of undress, primarily displaying rope, leather, or gags, though none showed a full face. Most were black and white, with a few in color sprinkled through. A few were even black and white with color showing only on the rope.

Two in particular caught his eye. One was a black-and-white close-up of wrists bound with bright red rope, the end of it draped between fingers. Another was the lower part of a man's face and neck, a hand resting on his throat from someone behind him, with two fingers of their other hand pressed against the man's lower lip.

Jasper paused in front of them for a long moment, resisting the urge to press a hand to his own throat. He knew from experience that it wouldn't feel the same as Vincent's hand on him.

He turned and continued walking as the achromatic bodies gave way to brilliant bursts of colors. One entire wall was dedicated to nature and was full of shots of the forest, with brilliant streaks of golden morning sunlight shining through trees or sunsets glimmering red and purple on the water. Sharp close-ups of various insects followed. Caterpillars and butterflies, a praying mantis, ladybugs, a giant fuzzy bee covered in pollen. A coiled red snake with stripes of black slightly hidden beneath a large rock.

"These are amazing," he said softly, turning to find Ash picking up a camera.

"Master Vincent suggested I take a few photos of you now, if you're willing."

Jasper swallowed and glanced at the pictures of the bodies again. "Do I need to be naked?"

Ash tilted his head and followed Jasper's gaze. "Skin is the most natural self, but no. Whatever you are comfortable with."

He gripped the hem of his shirt with a deep breath before unbuttoning another two buttons to show off more of the Shibari rope Vincent put so much effort into. "Is like this okay?"

Ash's lips twitched with a hint of a smile. He nodded and motioned across the room to a clear spot in front of a white backdrop, then turned on a few lights with umbrellas behind them.

Jasper stood in front of them and squinted until Ash adjusted the heights and angles so they weren't blinding him.

"Relax," Ash said, though that was easier said than done; the only photos ever taken of him were for school. Jasper blinked up at Ash when he stepped closer. "May I?" he asked, motioning to Jasper's shirt.

"Um, sure."

Ash tugged open a couple more buttons so only two were left, adjusted the shirt a bit to bare more of Jasper's right shoulder, and nudged it open to show off the ropes that went all the way to his hips. He cupped Jasper's wrists and lifted the left above his head and the right to grip the front of his shirt. Then he stepped back and raised the camera to snap a few pictures.

Jasper felt ridiculous, but then Ash quietly asked him to tilt his head down and to the side as the camera clicked again, and then to lick his lips, and something released inside him. He'd already seen for himself that Ash took amazing photos. Surely he wouldn't be wasting his time taking pictures of Jasper if he didn't think they would turn out good.

A few minutes later he was slipping his shirt off, following Ash's soft directions and pausing with the shirt bunched around his elbows and waist. He turned with his back to Ash and let it slowly slip to the floor. It was… strangely liberating. He'd never stripped and been the sole focus of someone's attention without sex being involved.

The click of the camera turned almost soothing, and he even started to enjoy himself. Striking poses like a model should have been absurd, but Ash didn't laugh or tell him to stop, merely offered the occasional suggestion and kept taking pictures from various angles and distances.

By the time Vincent and Zach joined them, Jasper had completely lost track of time, the cold of the basement forgotten beneath the heat of the lights and warmth of exertion. A stronger heat flooded him when he realized he'd even gotten his jeans unbuttoned with a teasing glimpse of boxers showing.

Zach wolf whistled, and Jasper shot him a scowl over his shoulder even as he heard the distinctive click of the camera. Zach smirked at him. "Oh, I want a copy of that one," he said as he slipped his arm around Ash's waist. "Well? You interested in an actual photo shoot?"

Jasper glanced at Vincent before picking up his shirt. "Maybe?" He slipped the shirt back on and stepped in against Vincent's side.

"I'll call you tomorrow," Vincent said, hooking a finger in the back loop of Jasper's jeans to tug him around.

"Sure. Nice meeting you, Jas."

"You too," he called and waved over his shoulder as Vincent urged him up the stairs. He wasn't able to get more than a step ahead when Vincent kept hold of him, and he snorted softly, wondering if Vincent had missed him for the short time he'd been downstairs or if he was horny after seeing Jasper partially undressed. He liked to think it was both.

The late afternoon heat was nearly stifling as they stepped outside and headed back to their own cabin. He hadn't noticed that so much time had passed. He glanced at Vincent from the corner of his eye. "They were nice."

"Yes." Vincent let out a slow breath and seemed to relax. "I'm glad you like them."

He smiled and hooked his arm around Vincent's waist, leaning into him as they walked, and he realized he'd finally met some of Vincent's *actual* friends.

Chapter 14

Vincent didn't realize exactly how worried he was about Jasper meeting Zach and Ash until Zach sang Jasper's praises and Ash was comfortable enough to show Jasper his studio. That Jasper seemed to get along with both of them in return was a relief.

And then seeing him half naked, the photo lights reflecting off of and highlighting the Shibari, the loose and relaxed set of his shoulders, and the smile as he enjoyed himself. A lesser man might have been jealous and insecure enough to take that jealousy out on Jasper, but Vincent turned that energy into an intense scene in the playroom.

He strapped Jasper down on the bench, reddened his ass, and slowly tormented him with a larger dildo than usual until he was begging. Jasper had only a few minutes to cool down when Vincent guided them upstairs to the bed, where he proceeded to take Jasper apart, murmuring Zach's and his own praises into his boy's ear while slowly and steadily fucking him.

Tears of desperate pleasure stained Jasper's cheeks by the time he finally came with a hoarse shout, and he was out cold almost before Vincent found his own release.

Cleaning up was easy enough—Jasper hadn't been in any state to make a choice on using condoms—and a few moments later Vincent followed him into sweet oblivion.

Until a phone started ringing.

He rolled over with a bleary grumble, silently cursing whichever of them had left their phone on, before he realized it wasn't either of their ringtones. That was enough, and he finally sat up. It was the landline downstairs ringing, but by the time he got out of bed, it stopped. He was debating going back to sleep when it started again a few seconds later.

With a grumble he stumbled down the stairs, clutching the banister for balance as his eyes adjusted. Despite the faint light from the balcony doors, he still managed to stub his toe on the table and finally snatched the receiver with a snarled, "Yes?"

"Hey," Zach said, sounding far too awake for three in the morning. "Sorry to wake you. I have an Amber calling our main line trying to reach you. Says it's an emergency."

Vincent swore softly as he woke completely. "I'll call her on her cell."

"Thanks."

Vincent hung up and flipped on the kitchen light to find his phone. It took a moment to boot up, and as soon as it did, he was flooded with texts and missed calls. He ignored them and moved to the far end of the kitchen as he called Amber.

She answered on the first ring. "Where's Jasper?"

"Asleep." Like any sane person would be, though he kept that thought to himself.

"I need to talk to him. Now, Vincent," she snapped.

He straightened with a sneer, his instinct for protecting Jasper warring against the societal expectation of giving ground to family. Considering they were several states away and no emergency could be solved with a single phone call, he sided with his instincts. "He's asleep after an intense scene. I won't interrupt his aftercare when there's nothing he can do about whatever you're calling for."

She was silent for long enough he suspected she was more upset at being denied than she was looking out for Jasper, though maybe that was the sleep deprivation making him more callous. "His father is in the hospital."

Vincent propped against the wall and pinched the bridge of his nose. Form what little Jasper had told him of his father, the man was an abusive asshole, but that wasn't a guarantee that Jasper wouldn't want to go home. "How bad?"

"Late-stage cancer. He's stable for the moment, but.... They're not sure he'll last past the week."

He blew out a slow breath. "I'll have him call you in the morning." He ended the call and immediately dialed his grandfather as he mentally ticked off things he needed to take care of before he woke Jasper. At least it was a reasonable hour in London.

"Thornwell residence" came Rupert's familiar accent. The man had worked as his grandparents' manservant for the past several decades and had saved Vincent's life a dozen times over while he'd been living overseas.

"Rupert. It's Vincent."

"Master Vincent, a pleasure," he replied with genuine warmth. "A bit early for you to be calling. Is aught all right?"

"Unfortunately not," Vincent said. "I was hoping I could borrow the jet."

Rupert was too professional to ask, but Vincent could hear the concern in his voice when he said, "One moment."

After a minute ticked by, Vincent gave up standing in the kitchen. The couch was close enough to the loft he'd risk waking Jasper, so he headed to the playroom and settled on the love seat there instead. While he waited he double-checked the flight times to make sure it wouldn't be faster to buy a last-minute ticket, but with the layovers and boarding hassles, the arrival times weren't much different. And the convenience of having a plane to themselves tipped the scales.

When the line reconnected his grandfather Arthur answered. "Vincent. So sorry about that. I was in a meeting. What's wrong?"

It didn't take long to explain the situation, though he left a lot of the details vague, and not much longer than that to have a promise for the jet to be waiting for them late that afternoon.

"You could have asked to use it in the first place."

Vincent smiled faintly. "It's not exactly my style."

"Just like your mother," Arthur said but without the disparaging disapproval that his grandmother would have employed. "Not exactly your style to take a vacation either, hmm?"

"I'm visiting friends. You remember Zach and Aston."

"By yourself?" The knowing tone nearly had Vincent rolling his eyes, and it was utterly ridiculous to be embarrassed about seeing someone when he was in his third decade. "They were planning to start a rather risqué business, if I remember correctly."

Vincent smothered a soft snort at that understatement. "No, not alone… I'm here with the man I'm seeing. It's his father in the hospital."

"What's he like? Better than that wanker you left here with, I hope."

Christ, how had he been so blind when everyone else saw how toxic Adam was? "It's only been a few months, but so far he's amazing."

"Good. Maybe you'll bring him to visit soon."

Vincent suspected Jasper would have an aneurysm if he saw the Thornwell estate. It wasn't quite as big as one that would be in a Jane Eyre rendition, but it was sizable. His grandmother wasn't exactly a selling point either. She liked to pretend his being gay was an immature indulgence or a phase he'd grow out of and spent his entire time living there continuously trying to set him up with the daughters of prominent families.

"We'll see."

They spent a few more minutes catching up before Arthur was called away to another meeting.

Vincent slumped and rested his head against the back of the love seat to stare blankly at the ceiling. He'd only gotten a couple hours of sleep, but he doubted he'd get more at this point. He sent a quick text to Zach letting him know they might be leaving early, but that he didn't have details yet. Packing wouldn't take long. The food was an issue, but Zach and Ash would put it to good use if they did leave.

For now he was stuck in a waiting game. He could have woken Jasper, but when he got a text from Rupert with the flight plan confirmation, he saw the jet wouldn't be there until nearly four that afternoon. Plenty of time for Jasper to make a decision and take care of everything after.

With a sigh he pushed himself up and headed back to the kitchen to caffeinate for the long day ahead.

CHAPTER 15

JASPER STIRRED awake to fingers combing through his hair and immediately wiggled closer to Vincent with a groan of protest. "No," he grumbled, rubbing his face against Vincent's shirt and breathing in the scent of warm skin and a lingering hint of soap.

"No, what?"

"No get up," Jasper whined and refused to open his eyes, even though he really should have been up before Vincent to make breakfast. Except if Vincent wanted breakfast in bed, he shouldn't have tormented Jasper for hours last night.

Vincent pressed a lingering kiss to his temple. "Sorry, pet, but you do need to get up."

He let out a heartfelt groan and threw a leg over Vincent's hip. "Why?"

Vincent sighed, his hand pausing in its path down Jasper's back. "Amber called."

Jasper grunted and pressed his face into Vincent's chest. "So? We're on vacation." Even as he said it, he knew that wasn't going to make a difference. She wouldn't have called for something trivial, and Vincent certainly wouldn't be making a big deal about it if it was.

"Pet," Vincent said, his voice soft, and Jasper instinctively tensed up enough even his lungs stopped working for a moment. "Your father is in the hospital."

Jasper wasn't sure how he should react to that. A small part of him thought *Good*! But the rest of him was apathetic. He didn't exactly wish his father ill so much as he tried not to let the asshole take up space in his head. "So?"

Vincent was silent for a long moment before his hand started moving again, a soothing rhythm that nearly made Jasper want to crawl out of his skin. "It sounds like he may not make it."

"Then there's no point in worrying about it. Or calling her back."

"You don't have to," Vincent replied slowly. "I'll tell her you don't want to talk to her. Does that mean you don't want to go back?"

"I want to stay here."

"Okay."

Jasper bit his tongue against asking if that was really okay. It was fine. He didn't want to see his father, and if he died it was likely because he'd been a drunken bastard for most of his life.

"So I'm going to tell her you don't want to talk right now. And that you're thinking about what to do," Vincent said after a moment. "You don't have to change your decision, but I did make arrangements for a flight back this evening in case you do."

He wouldn't, but he didn't bother saying so. He pulled back and rolled over to bury himself under the covers. He didn't care. His father had made it clear how much of a nuisance and disappointment Jasper was. Why should he have to give up the first vacation he'd ever had because the asshole might die?

When Amber took him in, his father never once called him to see where he'd gone or if he was coming back. Jasper assumed Amber had informed him at some point, but it'd been over a year since he'd last seen or spoken to his father.

He tugged the covers tighter when he heard Vincent speaking downstairs.

"No, he doesn't want to speak to you. He's awake. Yes, I told him. I'll let you know when he makes a decision. No. No," he repeated, sounding more than a little aggravated. "He's an adult. He can—" Vincent snarled softly a few moments before he started up the stairs.

Jasper heaved a sigh and sat up, not at all surprised she wasn't taking no for an answer. Even if she'd let Jasper move in, she didn't know the full extent of his father's neglect. Or pretended not to.

"She wants to hear from you," Vincent said softly, putting the phone on Speaker and holding it towards Jasper.

He almost took the offer of being a coward, but dealing with her in a week would be bad enough without adding not speaking to her now on his list of offenses. He took the phone from Vincent and turned off the speaker. At Vincent's questioning look, Jasper shook his head and waited for him to go back downstairs before staring at the phone and the call-duration time ticking up. He finally lifted it to his ear and said, "I don't want to talk."

"Jas," Amber said, exasperated and harried. There were muffled voices in the background and the faint squeak of shoes on linoleum.

"You need to come to the hospital. There's a flight leaving at one. I already bought the tickets for you. I sent Vincent all the info."

"Does he want to see me?"

"What—"

"Does he even want to see me," he repeated slower, enunciating every word.

"Of course he wants to see you."

Jasper scoffed. "Sure. Let me hear him say it, then."

"He's asleep right now."

"Then call me back when he wakes up."

"Get on the plane, Jasper! You can talk to him when you get here."

Jasper sneered and resisted the urge to find a hammer to break the phone into pieces. "No."

"What the fuck do you mean, no?"

"I'm not coming back just because he might die."

"He *is* dying," she snapped. "The cancer's already spread everywhere. There's nothing they can do but make him comfortable."

"Which is more than he deserves," he said before he could stop himself.

"Jasper Paulos Saris!"

He jabbed the End Call button and tossed the phone aside. It immediately started ringing, but he ignored it. Then ignored it again the next two times.

Five minutes later, he finally got sick enough of the ringing to answer, and she didn't give him time to say a word before ripping into him. "Stop being selfish! Vincent can take you on another vacation whenever you want. Your father is on his deathbed, and you will be here by tonight!"

"Or what?" he asked tightly, struggling against the painful racing of his heart.

A beat of silence followed before she answered. "Or you can find a new living arrangement."

"You're a fucking bitch, Amber. Stop calling." He threw the phone aside and stalked downstairs to the balcony. The near-stifling heat did nothing for his desire to scream, but he held it in. What peace and happiness he'd found the past several days was utterly obliterated now, and the guilt wriggling its way through him only made it worse.

He hated that he felt even a shred of guilt for not wanting to go back. Sharing blood didn't mean anything. If it did, Amber's family should have been there after his mother died, but those long years after her death, Jasper had only had his brother. Until he disappeared too.

He slumped against the railing and stared out at the trees. The wild flowers planted around the cabin were blooming, but their mild floral scent was more irritating than soothing. He bristled when the door slid open behind him. "Tell her to fuck off."

"I did."

Jasper blinked and hesitantly glanced over his shoulder. Vincent was still standing inside as if afraid of getting too close, and Jasper suddenly felt like an ass. "And I still don't want to go back."

"You don't have to."

Jasper squinted. "You're not going to try to make me?"

"You can make your own decisions. But I am going to make you come eat something."

He pushed off the railing with a huff. "Rather eat you," he muttered on his way by.

"I'm sure that can be arranged at some point," Vincent replied, and Jasper almost smiled at the audible eye roll. He dropped into a chair at the dining table, but even Vincent's gourmet scrambled eggs failed to entice his hunger. He sat poking at them as Vincent ate and drank coffee, and then Vincent's phone chimed with a text. Jasper looked up despite himself, the furrow between Vincent's brows not boding well.

"She's saying your brother is going to contact you on your phone."

Jasper shoved his untouched eggs away and went in search of his phone. He found it where it had fallen off the nightstand and sat on the bed to wait for it to turn on, then waited another several minutes before a text came through.

All it said was *You don't have to come.*

He stared at the words long enough the phone dimmed twice before he texted back. *Are you?*

Nah gonna get some champagne to celebrate

What'd amb say to that?

Fuck you not that stupid baby bro

A soft snort escaped Jasper, and he fell to lie on his side, absently flipping the phone over and over in his hand. The guilt was still there, somehow worse now that he knew Noah wouldn't be there either. Not that he'd expected otherwise. If Jasper's shitty childhood was a bad dream, Noah's had been a nightmare.

The kitchen sink turned on, and he focused on the running water and clink of dishes. That should have been him cleaning up. He tossed his phone on the nightstand and rolled over, curling up on his side as the guilt threatened to eat him alive. How long was Vincent willing to take over Jasper's duties before he got fed up?

Of course that bastard had one foot in the grave and was still finding ways to fuck up Jasper's life.

He pressed his face into the pillow with a long whine. This wasn't fair. He shouldn't be feeling guilty about not going back, or about wanting to stay here on his first vacation with Vincent. They were finally seeing each other for more than a couple of days a week, and it was amazing. If this was anything like how living with Vincent would be, he wanted more, but even daring to think that was enough that he let out another whine.

No way would Vincent want Jasper all up in his business all day every day. Except he wasn't going to have a place to live soon if Amber stood by her threat. He sure as hell couldn't ask to move in, but surely Vincent would let him stay while he figured out something more permanent.

"Pet."

Jasper froze and tugged the pillow down enough to eye Vincent where he stood at the top of the stairs. "Sex?" he asked hopefully. Not that he was in the mood, but he'd welcome any distraction at this point.

Vincent raised an eyebrow. "Is that really what you want right now?"

"Maybe. No? I don't know." Jasper made a face and flopped back on the bed with an exaggerated sigh.

Vincent took a step forward before pausing. "Would you rather be left alone?"

Jasper automatically opened his mouth to say yes, but the word wouldn't form. He wrapped his arms tight around the pillow instead and shook his head.

A moment later Vincent had closed the distance between them, the bed shifting as he sat and propped himself against the headboard.

Once he was settled, Jasper pushed the pillow away and replaced it with Vincent's chest, pressing his face into the sleep-worn shirt. Neither of them spoke, and he closed his eyes as Vincent stroked his hair. He tried to go back to sleep so he could wake up and pretend to start the day over, but the silence finally became too much.

"She bought plane tickets," he muttered.

"I saw," Vincent said, still running his fingers through Jasper's hair, his other hand resting on the arm thrown over his stomach.

"I don't want to leave."

"We don't have to."

He clutched Vincent's shirt. "Really?"

Vincent paused his stroking and curled his fingers tight for a moment, tingles of pleasure sparking along Jasper's scalp. "I can't make this choice for you. Whatever you decide, I'll support you either way. Even if it pisses off your family."

Jasper swallowed hard. "You don't think I'm being selfish?"

"No." Vincent dragged his fingers to the back of Jasper's neck. "In my experience, selfish is a word entitled people throw around when they don't get their way." He dug his thumb into a knot on Jasper's shoulder. "It's not selfish to protect yourself. I don't know anything about your relationship other than he was abusive."

Jasper blinked against the prickling in his eyes. How was it fair that someone he'd only known a few months cared more about him than his own family? He took several slow breaths until he didn't feel like he'd shatter into pieces anymore, though it didn't help the choking sensation from all the words trying to escape. Talking about his father was the absolute last thing he wanted to do, but the day was already ruined. Fuck, probably the rest of the week, and the rest of the vacation too. How could he possibly enjoy himself now?

"He used to lock us in our room on the weekends," he murmured. "Said we were too loud. Then he turned up the TV so he couldn't hear us." Vincent squeezed his arm but didn't speak, and Jasper couldn't stand the silence. "Would punish Noah whenever he got bad grades. He broke Noah's arm when he got an F, but then some woman came around and started asking questions, and he switched to the belt."

Somehow that had been worse, but then Noah took off the moment he graduated, and Jasper was left to deal with their father alone. He'd been old enough by then he could mostly fend for himself, and a locked door was more a blessing than a punishment. He'd expected to take his brother's place with the belt and groundings, but he only ever caught his father's attention when the bastard was drunk.

He'd chalked it up to the fact he'd kept his grades up and had learned to live silently. It wasn't until Noah called one evening needing bail money that he'd overheard his father tell Noah he wasn't his kid and to never call again. At first he'd thought that meant because Noah was an adult and not his legal responsibility anymore. It was only later that Jasper realized he'd meant it as literal truth when his father was drunk and muttering about finally being rid of "that bastard's bastard."

Exhaustion seeped through Jasper when he finished explaining all this to Vincent, though he couldn't ignore the relief that came with it. He'd never told anyone about any of that before. He'd never even noticed the weight of the secrets until some of it eased away.

"You don't owe it to him to be there," Vincent said quietly when the silence stretched between them. "And you don't owe anyone an explanation on why. But you do owe it to yourself to consider if there's anything you want to say to him before you no longer have the chance."

Jasper scoffed and burrowed closer. "Like what? Thanks for ruining my life, Dad?"

"If that's something you want to get off your chest."

"No…." He didn't have much of anything he wanted to say. He didn't even care about the why. He vaguely remembered his parents before his mother died, and he preferred to think it was her death that changed him. "I just don't want to feel guilty for not going." Or to lose his home, but even he knew better than to say that aloud.

"Not sure I can help with that."

Jasper groaned and crawled completely on top of Vincent. "What good are you, then?" he grumbled.

"Not much it seems."

He grunted and bit Vincent's shoulder, then let out a frustrated whine. "We should go back," he muttered, but he made no effort to move.

"Is that what you want to do?"

"No, but Amber will be a bitch if I don't."

"Forget Amber for the moment."

Jasper made a face and rolled off Vincent to stare at the ceiling. "You don't live with her." Vincent's curious hum almost distracted Jasper enough to get his hopes up, but he refused to stress about his living situation until he had to. "We could… come back after?" he asked softly. It was ridiculous to even think that was possible. He didn't know how much Vincent had already spent on this cabin or the tickets, but it was too much.

Before he could try to take it back Vincent replied. "We could. We still have the cabin for over a week."

A different guilt twisted through Jasper's chest, but he tried to shove it down. Tried to tell himself this was his birthday gift. That if Vincent wasn't willing to spend the money on tickets, he wouldn't have offered. "I'll pay you back," he blurted, then winced. He barely had enough money to cover emergency necessities as it was.

"It won't cost me anything," Vincent said, earning a sharp look from Jasper.

"Why won't it?"

Vincent cleared his throat. "I requested to borrow my grandfather's private jet in case you decided to go back. It'll be here late this afternoon."

Jasper pushed onto his elbows to stare at Vincent. "You did what now? Wait, when did you find out?" The way Vincent refused to meet his eye probably should have been concerning, but Jasper was more interested in the fact that Vincent seemed nervous. It was such a rare phenomenon he almost wanted to take a picture.

"About three this morning."

"Why didn't you wake me then?"

"Because it wouldn't have changed anything aside from you not getting sleep. Even if you wanted to return today, the earliest flight we could have made is the one Amber bought tickets for this afternoon."

"Have you been awake since three?"

"More or less."

That wouldn't do.

Jasper shifted back and grabbed the pillow to whack Vincent in the chest with. "Take a nap."

Vincent slanted a bemused look at him. "I'm fine."

"I don't care. Nap with me."

With an exaggerated sigh, Vincent stretched out on the bed, then turned to Jasper and raised an eyebrow in a silent *Are you happy now*?

Jasper tucked himself back in against Vincent's side and willed himself back to sleep. It didn't work, but at least he had an excuse not to do anything or even think for a while. Hopefully he'd know what to do by the time Vincent woke up.

In the end, Jasper caved.

As much as he had no desire to see his father, the guilt wouldn't leave him, and Amber kept messaging Vincent demanding an answer.

Why she cared so much was beyond him. It wasn't like he was invested much in the health of *her* parents. He hadn't even seen them since he was a kid. If he only showed up for half an hour, he hoped that would still be enough that she would let him get back to his vacation and enjoy the next week in peace.

He insisted on leaving their things. More for a sense of conviction that they'd come back than for a reasonable excuse to leave home quickly, but there was that too.

For some reason he expected a small plane barely bigger than a helicopter that only seated a few people with no leg room. Instead he found himself sitting next to Vincent on a plane half the size of the one they flew in on. Plenty of room to move, and some of the seats even turned into beds.

His phone went off with a text alert, and as much as he didn't want to read it, he pulled it up anyway.

The one-word text from Noah was a simple *Seriously?*

Not staying long

Just long enough to get Amber off their backs.

Whatever was followed a few moments later by *Now she's harassing me as the bad son so thanks for that*

Jasper winced and typed out several messages but deleted each one. Noah should tell Amber the truth, but Jasper couldn't say that; he wasn't supposed to know they were half brothers. Hell, he didn't even know for sure if Noah knew, or if he'd taken their father's words figuratively too. He couldn't very well tell Noah to come, either, so he settled for what he wished he could do himself. *Tell her to fuck off*

Lol I might

When no more messages came through, he tossed his phone aside and stared out the window. "I can't believe you really have a private plane."

"It's not mine," Vincent replied without looking up from his phone.

Jasper rolled his eyes and leaned over to find Vincent reserving a rental car from the airport. He bit his tongue against the apology burning his throat, but he could only hold it back for so long. "Sorry," he whispered when Vincent had paid and switched to his emails.

Instead of telling him it was fine—again—Vincent tipped Jasper's chin up and planted a slow chaste kiss against his lips.

Jasper leaned into him with a long whine. "Why did I think leaving was a good idea?"

Vincent shook his head with a soft huff and turned back to his phone. "Should I tell the pilot to turn around?"

He whined again and flopped across Vincent's lap. "No…." He could do this. Chances of his father even caring or wanting to see him were slim, and then Amber could see for herself how much of an asshole he really was.

BY THE time they landed and found the rental car it was getting late, and as much as Jasper wanted to go straight to the hospital so they could turn around and leave again, Vincent said the earliest time they could fly back would be tomorrow afternoon. Instead of telling Amber to fuck off like he desperately wanted, he ignored her texts telling him his father was awake and to come despite the hour.

He'd barely eaten anything for lunch and still wasn't hungry, at least until Vincent stopped to pick up food from a restaurant. Jasper hadn't even noticed him ordering food. He sat holding the bag, breathing in the warm scent of tomatoes and garlic and basil. His stomach rumbled and his mouth watered in anticipation the entire fifteen-minute drive to Vincent's home.

Even though his nose didn't lie, seeing the spaghetti when he opened one of the containers still made his chest squeeze tight. They could have easily picked up fast food, but he refused to read more into it than Vincent choosing decent food over a burger joint.

He dropped into a chair and dug in, all but inhaling the noodles and garlic bread, plus the extra piece Vincent dropped into his container at some point. When he'd finished eating, he wasn't quite as ready to bite the head off the next person who texted him. "Thanks," he said softly, "but it wasn't as good as yours."

Vincent slanted him an amused look, and Jasper managed a cheeky grin even if it only lasted a few seconds. Once Vincent was done, Jasper gathered everything up to toss in the trash, then let Vincent tug him to the sofa, where he started a movie Jasper had added to their watch list.

Ten minutes in and Jasper slumped against Vincent's side, blinking hard to stay awake. He didn't remember losing the fight, but he woke up to Vincent nudging him.

"I can't carry you up the stairs, pet."

He grumbled in protest but stumbled up the stairs after Vincent, barely managing to get his pants off before face-planting on the bed.

Chapter 16

VINCENT SLEPT later than usual. Seven was still too early, but when the fiery nightmares occasionally woke him only a few hours after closing his eyes, he'd take what he could get.

Jasper was still out cold, so Vincent lazed a bit longer, mentally preparing himself for the day, or more likely days, to come. If Jasper's father was really in as bad shape as Amber said, they might not make it back to the cabin. Or even if they did, they'd still have to cut their vacation short. That would be disappointing, but he breathed through the irritation of having his plans interrupted.

Nothing he could do would change the situation. He'd done what he could to ensure Jasper was able to come back and hoped he got whatever answers or closure he needed. The only thing Vincent could do now was support Jasper, since it seemed his family was unable or unwilling to do that.

He'd suspected before that Jasper's living arrangements weren't ideal, merely the best he had available. Vincent could easily fix that, had already resisted the urge to do so a few times. But he worried a few months was far too soon to suggest living together. Or to provide Jasper with living accommodations, even if that thought made him feel like a pimp. He could give Jasper that if he needed it, though.

Minutes ticked into an hour, and then into two, and Vincent drifted back to sleep before Jasper stirred. He cracked an eye open when Jasper rolled over to octopus on to him.

"Do we have to get up?"

"Eventually." Vincent slipped his hand under Jasper's shirt and spread his fingers against his sleep-warm back. "Are you hungry?"

"Not really."

"What can you stomach eating?"

"Spaghetti."

Vincent snorted and lightly swatted Jasper's ass. "Anything else?"

Jasper sighed as if he'd been told he had an essay due tomorrow. "I guess I could eat some toast."

"Toast it is." He would have gotten up then, but Jasper tightened his grip and refused to budge. "Changing your mind?" he asked after a long moment.

"No… I didn't come all the way back for nothing."

Vincent held his tongue against offering Jasper the choice to return to the cabin. If Jasper's guilt had brought him this far, it'd be better for it to play out. He wasn't willing to risk leaving in case that guilt got the better of him again. Instead he rolled to his side and pulled Jasper flush against himself. "Do you want to set a time to leave for today or wait and see after the visit?"

Jasper didn't answer for long enough that Vincent suspected he'd fallen back asleep, but then he said, "Can you decide?"

"I can," he replied slowly. He didn't mind making whatever decisions Jasper needed, especially if he was overwhelmed. "In that case you go shower while I start breakfast."

Jasper squeezed his arms even tighter and took a few deep breaths before letting go and crawling out of bed.

Vincent scrubbed a hand over his face, got ready for the day, and headed to the kitchen. The last of the bread had molded in the short time they'd been gone, so he tossed it and checked the fridge. There were a few eggs left that were still good, and the waffle mix would hopefully be an acceptable substitute for toast.

Jasper took longer than usual in the shower, and his hair was still dripping when he finally sat at the table. He poked at his food, but he dutifully took a few bites here and there.

They ate in silence, and Vincent waited for him to decide he didn't actually want to go, but when no protest was forthcoming, he got them on the road. It was a short drive to the hospital, where Vincent led them up to the room number Amber had texted him.

He wasn't quite prepared for the uncomfortable dread crawling along his nerves at being inside a hospital again, but he ignored it as best he could.

When they found the room, he knocked twice and cracked the door open, spotting Amber in a chair on the far side before stepping back to let Jasper in.

Jasper took two steps in and stopped, his body rigid. "I'm here. Happy now?" he muttered, looking anywhere but at the bed.

Vincent propped the door open and stood behind Jasper as he studied the sleeping, emaciated man lying on the bed. He had the same brown skin and blond hair as Jasper, but that was the only resemblance he could find.

"You should have been here yesterday," Amber said, sitting up from the makeshift bed she'd put together against the windowsill.

Jasper flinched back half a step. "I didn't want to come to begin with," he hissed.

"Yes, you made that abundantly clear," she replied with an annoyed glare. From the state of her hair and makeup, it was clear she'd been here a while.

Vincent didn't quite understand the dynamics, since as far as he understood, they were cousins through Jasper's mother, not his father. He pressed his hand against Jasper's lower back in silent support. "How long have you been here?" he asked.

Amber's frown deepened. "Since the day before yesterday."

"Alone?"

She waved her hand and reached up to pull her ponytail free. "Terrance brings me food and stays in the evenings after work," she said as she combed her hair with her fingers and put it back up. "Now that you're here, I'm going home to shower."

"Fuck that." Jasper pressed harder into Vincent's hand. "I'm not staying that long."

"Stop being so selfish," she snapped.

"That's enough," Vincent said, sliding his hand to Jasper's hip and squeezing.

She cut a glare at him. "You can stay out of it. This doesn't concern you."

Vincent raised an eyebrow, tightening his grip on Jasper's hip when he shifted as if he was going to lunge, and stared her down as he mentally counted to ten. "I'm going to assume that's sleep deprivation and stress talking."

Amber pressed her lips into a thin line, but when she didn't say anything else, he sighed. "We'll stay an hour," he said. Beside him Jasper tensed, but that was the least they could do after coming all this way. Even an hour felt too short, though considering the rough start, he expected Jasper to try to leave after a few minutes.

When she started to protest, Vincent cut her off. "One hour. Go shower and rest. And maybe send someone to take our place."

"There is no one else," she replied tightly as she grabbed her purse. "Jas and Noah are his only family." She leveled an expectant look on Jasper. "Call Noah and—"

"Shut up," Jasper said, hands clenched at his sides. "He has even less reason to be here than me. He's not coming, and we're not staying." He leaned into Vincent's side, where the faint tremors going through him ricocheted through both of them. "One hour."

Before she could respond, coughing interrupted them.

When Vincent turned to the bed, Jasper's father was awake and didn't seem particularly happy to see them. "Did you bring beer?" he rasped, hunching on his side as another coughing fit wracked him.

"Of course they didn't bring beer," Amber huffed.

The man collapsed back to the bed with labored breathing. "Worthless as usual," he muttered.

Jasper wrapped his arms over his stomach and leaned into Vincent hard enough he'd likely fall over if Vincent moved an inch. Vincent bristled and pulled him even closer. Before he could find an acceptable response, Amber stepped closer to the bed, her fists curled into fists.

"Are you shitting me? You're not even supposed to be drinking!" Vincent had to force his jaw to unclench when that turned out to be her only issue. "Whatever," she snapped. "Do what you want. I need to go home and shower and eat something that isn't half grease. Jasper will be here if you need anything."

"Don't bother," the man sneered. "I told you I don't need anyone here."

"Sure. We'll just leave you to the American healthcare system then, shall we?" Amber replied dryly. "I'm sure they won't screw up your meds while there's no witness."

He muttered under his breath, low enough Vincent couldn't catch anything but the scathing tone. Part of him had hoped this would at least be a civil visit, but now he wasn't sure he was willing to stay even a few more minutes, much less an hour.

"If you don't need us here, we'll go ahead and leave, then," Jasper said.

"Don't you dare," Amber hissed.

"Why not? You're the only one who gives a shit."

Vincent slid his hand up to Jasper's shoulder and gave a gentle squeeze, but Jasper twisted away from the touch.

"He doesn't even care that he's dying, why the fuck should I? Why do you? You never cared enough to come around after Mom died."

"That's not—"

"Why are you even here? It's not like you're related by blood."

Amber's wince was so slight Vincent might have missed it if he hadn't been watching her so closely. "Mom's still listed as his emergency contact."

"Then where is she?"

"Busy."

Jasper scoffed. "*I* was busy."

Vincent glanced at the bed to find Jasper's father watching him through narrowed eyes. Once he saw he had Vincent's attention, he demanded, "Who are you?"

"Vincent."

"Lawyer or something?"

Jasper spun to face the bed and lifted his chin. "My boyfriend."

The man's expression twisted with disgust. "Bad enough you don't bring me beer, now you're flaunting your faggotry? Good that your mother's dead or she'd kill herself from shame."

Vincent snarled as Jasper flinched like he'd been physically assaulted and stepped on Vincent's foot as he caught his balance. "Fuck. You," he said before Vincent could make the bad decision to punch the bedridden asshole in the face. Jasper grabbed Vincent's hand and hauled him out of the room as fast as he could without outright running.

Vincent squeezed tight and kept up, following Jasper's lead and ignoring Amber calling for them as they headed directly for the elevators. One opened for them immediately, but unfortunately she caught up to them before the doors closed, despite Vincent jabbing the button as soon as they stepped on. She stood facing them with her arms crossed as the elevator began its descent. When neither of them spoke, Vincent decided to pry for some of his own answers.

"Why would your mother be his emergency contact?"

Amber cast a furtive glance at Jasper before finding the corner of the elevator interesting enough to stare at. "They were having an affair at one point."

Jasper made a high noise of offense. "Excuse me?"

"As far as I know, they broke it off after the funeral."

"Did Mom know?"

Amber scoffed though quickly tried to disguise it as a cough. "Please. Your mother was no saint either. She had her own affair going with Dad."

"What?"

Vincent winced at the volume of Jasper's incredulous shout, but he couldn't exactly blame him for that reaction. Their family dynamics were even more fucked-up than his own.

"How long have you known?" Jasper asked.

"I don't know. Years."

"And you never said anything?" Jasper demanded.

"You were a kid. Why would I say anything?"

"You could have told me when I moved in! You've been lying to me this entire time."

Amber eyed him with so much condescension that Vincent took an instinctive step forward even as he fought against the urge to lash out. He hadn't been any help against Jasper's father, but he could at least keep Amber from doing any further damage.

"Unless you have anything of value to say, we're done here," Vincent said.

Amber shot him a dirty look, but the elevator slowed to a stop and the doors opened before she could say anything.

Jasper didn't wait for a response. As soon as he could slip through, he was gone, his bruising grip pulling Vincent behind. He didn't slow until they were out of the hospital and near the car, and then he rocked to a halt beside it. "She knew," he muttered, bracing his free hand above the window. "All this time, and she never said anything. Does she know about Noah?"

"Do you want to ask her?"

Jasper shook his head. "Not right now. I wanna go home."

Vincent knew better than to read anything into it, but he was pleased if wary at Jasper calling his place home. He unlocked the car and waited for Jasper to let go and get in before moving to the driver's side.

As he drove he wondered how long it would take Jasper to start asking if he and Noah were half brothers to Amber, rather than only cousins.

CHAPTER 17

JASPER WAS subdued the rest of the day, and Vincent gave him space, keeping close but not hovering. Most of the time Jasper spent sprawled on the sofa texting. Vincent couldn't help but be curious, though he held his tongue—at least until Jasper finally heaved a sigh and tossed his phone aside, where it clattered to the coffee table.

Vincent muted the TV show he wasn't really watching. "What's going on?"

Jasper sat up enough to slump against the arm of the sofa with an exaggerated groan, which was at least a little comforting. If he was back to his dramatics, he likely wasn't in shock, or worse, brooding. "Amber wants to talk to me and Noah."

"That sounds ominous."

He shot Vincent a wry smile, then rocked forward to crawl across the sofa and put his head in Vincent's lap.

"Are you going to talk to her?"

"I don't want to."

Vincent combed fingers through Jasper's hair with a soft hum. "Would you rather have it hanging over your head for the rest of our vacation?"

Jasper whined and pressed his face into Vincent's leg. "That's not fair."

"I think it's more than fair," Vincent replied. "I'd rather have you fully present when we get back to the cabin, not worrying about what she might say when you get home."

Jasper didn't respond for a long moment. "What if she says something terrible?"

"Like what?"

He shrugged and picked at Vincent's jeans over his knee. "Both my parents were apparently cheating whores. I guess it can't get much worse than that."

Vincent flexed his fingers tighter in a gentle tug. "Do you want to talk about it?"

Jasper shrugged again before rolling over. "I don't even remember her much," he said, his voice muffled where he'd pressed his face into Vincent's stomach. "But I thought she'd been happy. I thought they were both happy and loved each other, and that he only started drinking after Mom died because he didn't want to live without her."

"Those could all still be true."

Jasper scoffed. "They were both cheating on each other."

"That doesn't have to be mutually exclusive to everything else."

He pulled back enough to glare at Vincent with one eye. "Yes, it does."

Vincent raised an eyebrow and decided Jasper could keep being stubborn for the moment. "Okay."

"Okay." Jasper slumped into Vincent and blew out a long breath. "Can we go back to the cabin tonight if I talk to her now?"

"Possibly." Vincent picked up his phone to check his messages. Initially he'd planned to return to the cabin as soon as possible, but when Jasper got absorbed in texting, he held off in the hopes of some kind of resolution. Another day here was worth it if it meant they could properly enjoy the rest of their stay. "They can get a flight plan for two in the morning."

Jasper sat up and turned wide, pleading eyes on him.

"I'll get it booked. Why don't you call Amber, see if she and Noah can come for dinner?"

Jasper wrinkled his nose. "We're going to cook?"

"No." He wasn't feeling generous enough to cook for her after everything, and he certainly didn't want to deal with the dishes if they were leaving tonight. "Have her bring dinner."

Jasper nodded, quickly leaning in to press a kiss to Vincent's cheek before snatching up his phone. By the time Vincent got confirmation they could leave at two, Jasper had convinced Amber and Noah to come for dinner and bring food.

Whatever Amber had to say, Vincent could only hope it started mending things instead of causing more drama.

JASPER DIDN'T want to be here. Bad enough he was losing part of his alone time with Vincent. Now the one place he could find any sense of peace and quiet was being invaded. Worse, the food wasn't even good. Amber and the others loved the pizza place they always ordered from, but Jasper was sure its best flavor was nostalgia. Only drunk or over-caffeinated college students stressing over finals could tolerate wet-cardboard pizza crust and old grease.

Vincent had taken two pieces to his office to let them talk, and Jasper was stuck somewhere between relieved and betrayed. He managed two bites before giving up, eyeing Noah as he ate one slice after another like he hadn't eaten in days. Considering how much weight he'd lost since the last time Jasper saw him, that was likely closer to the truth than Jasper wanted to think about.

Maybe he'd gotten spoiled over the last year, especially the last few months. Ever since he met Vincent, the quality of the food he had access to was an entire galaxy better than what he'd grown up with. But time was ticking, and Amber had only taken a few bites of her first slice, with the air of someone eating their last meal.

"What's going on?" he finally asked, unable to keep quiet any longer.

Amber dropped her hands to her lap and glanced at Noah instead of answering. "You really won't go see him?"

Noah didn't look up from his pizza as his lip curled back in an impressive sneer. "He's not my father."

Jasper tensed and watched Noah from the corner of his eye, but Amber grunted softly, as if she'd expected that response. He narrowed his eyes at her. "You don't seem surprised."

"Funny," said Noah, "neither do you."

"I found out the same time you did."

"Oh yeah? When was that?"

"When you called from jail," Jasper admitted softly. He'd nearly taken the money from his father's wallet regardless in order to bail Noah out, but without a way to get to the jail, he'd been powerless to help. Noah studied him a moment before shrugging and turning back to finishing off the rest of both the large pizzas by himself.

"Did you really only call us both here to beg us to go to the hospital?" Jasper demanded. He shouldn't have been surprised, but he'd hoped that maybe, just maybe, she'd put what he wanted over what she thought was best. She'd been there earlier. No way could she be asking Jasper to deal with that bullshit again.

"No," she said softly, taking a breath as she straightened. "I was hoping you'd take a DNA test."

"To prove what? That we're half brothers? We already know that." Jasper sat back in his chair and crossed his arms.

"No. I want all three of us to take one."

Jasper stared at her as he waited for her to explain, but Noah responded before she did.

"Fuck you." Noah dropped the half-eaten crust of the last piece of pizza to his plate and sat back. "I don't care if we're more than cousins. Bit too late to give a shit about that, don't you think?"

"I need to know—"

"I don't."

"—if he's really my father!" Amber shouted over Noah.

"What?" She couldn't have meant that. She was older than both of them, though not much older than Noah. No way were their parents cheating on each other even before he was born.

Noah scoffed. "Like I said, bit too late to care. What are you hoping to get out of knowing now?"

"I just want to know the truth."

"No," Jasper said, shoving to his feet with a scraping of chair legs across the floor. "I don't want to know. You didn't grow up in that hellhole. Even if he's your biological father, it doesn't change anything."

Noah made a considering noise. "It could change some things."

Jasper rounded on him with an incredulous look. "Like what?"

Noah shrugged. "If it turns out I'm actually a bastard child of Uncle Gabe's, he'll have to add me to the inheritance."

"Of course you only want the money," Jasper muttered, pushing away from the table in disgust.

"Like you have any room to talk," Noah shot back.

"The fuck is that supposed to mean?"

Noah raised an eyebrow and waved a hand around at the dining room and rest of the house. "You've certainly moved up in the world."

"It's not like I live here."

"Why not?"

Jasper flinched and forced in a breath around the sudden tightness in his chest. Even if he'd fantasized about moving in, he'd only been with Vincent a few months. Didn't he have to wait at least a year to expect that? Even then, he wasn't sure he could even ask. The last thing he wanted was to become a burden or annoyance, or for Vincent to agree out of some sense of obligation, only to regret it later.

"None of your business."

Noah rolled his eyes and turned back to Amber. "Well?" he asked. "Sure you want to risk losing or sharing your money?"

"He wouldn't cut me off."

"Sure about that? Doubt you could afford to keep living in your mansion if he did," Noah taunted.

Jasper gripped the edge of the table for balance, unable to believe his ears. Did Noah want the money or not? If he'd suspected who his father was before now, why hadn't he done something when he got kicked out? Or when his arm was broken? Had he known back then? How could he have? They'd been kids. Even if he had known, what could he have done?

And why was Jasper the only one shocked to learn his mother and aunt had been cheating with each other's husbands? For a few moments he worried he was a by-product of incest before the logical part of his brain kicked in. His mother and aunt were sisters and married into vastly different families. It was still fucked-up but not as bad as it could have been, which was something he never thought he'd have to be grateful for.

Everything he thought he knew about his parents was a lie. What else was a lie? Were they even his parents, or had they found him in a box on the side of the road like an abandoned kitten? Why else would his father hate him so much?

"Jas!"

He flinched at the sudden grip of a hand on the back of his neck, then instinctively relaxed beneath it. He closed his eyes with a shuddering breath as Vincent's thumb traced a firm line behind his ear.

"Breathe," Vincent murmured, his other hand a warm weight on Jasper's arm.

After a long moment of silence, Amber cleared her throat. "We should go. Enjoy the rest of your vacation," she said, and maybe it was the shock still in his system, but she didn't even sound grudging when she said it.

Jasper dropped into his chair and covered his face with his hands as he finally got his breathing under control. When he heard the front door close he slumped into Vincent. "Can we leave now?" he asked softly. He wanted out of the house and the city. Away from his family.

"Give me ten minutes," Vincent said, squeezing Jasper's neck and arm before stepping away.

Jasper slumped against the table and listened to the clinking of dishes and running water as Vincent cleaned up. The guilt that fluttered in his stomach was short-lived enough that he stayed where he was until Vincent finished.

They headed out, and Jasper settled into the passenger seat while Vincent tossed the trash in the bin, and then they were off, back to the airport. They were early enough they had a couple of hours to kill.

Vincent sat them in a booth at a table in a lounge and slid a menu in front of Jasper.

That was enough to finally draw him out of the daze he'd fallen into, and he slanted a questioning look at Vincent. "How'd you know I didn't eat?"

"That pizza was terrible," Vincent replied, studying his own menu. "Do you want to talk about it?"

"The pizza?" Jasper picked at the corner of his menu with a brief smile. "Not really." If only he could forget the last two days had ever happened. "I'd rather not even think about any of it."

"Okay. Why don't we talk about what to do with our last week?"

Jasper leaned into Vincent as he skimmed the menu. "You mean we're going to do something other than have sex?" He doubted an airport would have decent food, even if the lounge was fancy enough it was likely reserved for first-class passengers, so he settled on chicken tenders and fries.

"Ash is willing to do a proper photo shoot if you're up for it."

Jasper couldn't stop the high sound that escaped his throat. "By proper, you mean naked."

"You can keep your underwear on."

He rolled his eyes and turned his head enough to gnaw on Vincent's bicep.

"I really should start putting a muzzle on you."

"Why would you do that? I wouldn't be able to put my mouth on you."

"Oh no," Vincent replied, completely deadpan. "However would I survive?"

"You wouldn't."

Vincent snorted and slipped his arm around Jasper's back, leaning in so his lips brushed his ear. "I'm sure I could find one to suit my needs."

Jasper shivered as heat bloomed low in his gut, though he managed a quiet, "You're such a dick, Sir."

"You like it." He pulled back when their food arrived.

Jasper tried not to be disappointed at the loss of contact and grabbed the ketchup. He ate his way through two chicken strips before propping his shoulder against Vincent. "We can do a photo shoot."

"You're sure?"

"Yeah." He liked Zach and Ash. It would be fun to hang out with them again, even if he was half naked. "Maybe we can do lunch again." He glanced up to find a soft smile on Vincent's face and suddenly found it hard to breathe. Vincent looked good like that. Younger. Not that he was that old, no matter how much Jasper liked to tease him otherwise. Even with the bit of scruff he'd let grow, he didn't appear thirty.

"I'm sure I can convince Zach to have us over again."

"Good." Jasper stole one of Vincent's onion rings, covered it in ketchup, and shoved the entire thing in his mouth. "Tell him I want his special mashed potatoes."

CHAPTER 18

IT WAS raining when they finally returned to the cabin, which suited Jasper fine. He wasn't much in the mood for anything other than passing out in bed. He'd managed to doze on the plane, but the last few days were finally catching up to him.

He kicked his shoes off inside the door and stripped his shirt off on the way up the stairs, then dropped his pants by the bed before face-planting into his pillow. He expected to finally slip into sweet unconsciousness but found himself listening to the thunder and rain and Vincent checking things downstairs instead.

A few moments later the air-conditioner kicked on, and he breathed a sigh of pleasure at the cool air blowing on his bare skin. He waited until Vincent made his way up and joined him in bed to roll over and wrap his limbs around Vincent. "Thank you," he murmured into Vincent's shoulder. "Even though it was a stupid waste of time."

"It wasn't," Vincent said, adjusting them so he could settle both arms around Jasper. "Even if it only eased your guilt, it was worth the trouble." He squeezed Jasper's shoulders and pressed a kiss to the top of his head.

"Sorry you had to meet him."

"I'm sorry you had to grow up with that."

Jasper burrowed closer and breathed in the lingering scent of Vincent's cologne. How had he gotten lucky enough to catch Vincent's interest? More importantly, how could he possibly keep it for months, let alone years or… decades? At some point this would all come to an end, wouldn't it?

"What are you worrying about?"

Jasper was too exhausted to censor his response. "Us."

Vincent turned his head and blew a sleepy sigh into Jasper's hair. "What about us?"

"Just wondering how long this can last."

"Ah."

When that was his only response, Jasper curled his fingers tighter into the back of Vincent's shirt. "I like you. I like spending time with you." He didn't want this to ever end, but he at least caught himself before he could say that out loud.

"I do too, pet." Vincent rubbed his palm against Jasper's back. "I can't promise how long it'll last, but I have no intention of letting you go anytime soon."

It wasn't much of a promise, but it was enough for now. Jasper hadn't irreparably ruined their vacation, and Vincent didn't want to end their contract early. As he finally drifted to sleep, Jasper told himself not to worry about their time together until their current contract neared its end.

Chapter 19

VINCENT WOULD never admit it, but he was relieved to be back in the cabin. He'd known Jasper's father had to be a piece of work, but seeing it for himself was worse than his imagination. He wasn't too impressed with Amber, either, though he supposed family had a tendency to bring out the worst in each other. It didn't make it any easier to keep from offering to let Jasper move into his spare bedroom.

The last person he'd lived with was Adam, and that was only after dating him for their final year at Oxford. Looking back, even that had been too soon, but that likely had more to do with Adam being a toxic asshole and Vincent ignoring everyone around him trying to tell him as much. The fact both Zach and Ash had taken to Jasper should have been enough to quell any doubts, but Jasper moving in would hopefully mean wearing Vincent's collar and an entirely new level to their relationship.

Not that he didn't want that. Jasper had already proven to be an amazing sub, and they worked well together, but were they really ready for that kind of commitment? Jasper was still young, still in college, likely hadn't even reached the point of fully realizing who he was or wanted to be yet. None of which were deal breakers, but they weren't to be ignored either.

Jasper shifted in his sleep, rolling away from the streak of watery sunlight filtering through the blinds. He curled closer to Vincent, most of his warm olive skin exposed where he'd kicked the covers off in the night.

Vincent draped the sheet over him as the AC turned on with a rush of cool air, content to watch Jasper sleep for a few minutes before finally getting up to start the day. He needed a shower, but if Jasper was still in the mindset of wanting Vincent to make decisions for him, he had plans for how to accommodate.

He settled for wiping a warm cloth over his face and neck, then headed down to start breakfast. While the pans warmed he grabbed his phone, glad to see no missed calls from Amber. A text from Zach confirmed they were free to have lunch whenever, and that Ash could do the photo shoot as soon as the rain let up.

He got the eggs and bacon started and then checked the forecast. The rain was supposed to last all day, but the rest of the week should be clear. He suggested two days out for the shoot, to give the ground a chance to dry up, and lunch the day after. A thumbs-up response came through a few minutes later, and he set his phone aside to focus on cooking.

Jasper stumbled into the kitchen like a zombie as Vincent was finishing the first pancake and plastered himself to Vincent's back. "Not allowed to leave me alone in bed," he grumbled, wrapping his arms tight around Vincent's stomach.

"My mistake. I'll be sure to wake you next time I'm up before dawn," he replied dryly.

"Why would you be up before dawn?" Jasper asked, his words warped by a loud yawn. "Only psychos get up that early."

"Who says I'm not?" Vincent grabbed a plate and pried one of Jasper's hands free to press the dish into. "Eat up."

Jasper made a happy noise. "Am I going to need my strength?"

He leaned over to steal a quick kiss. "Always," he murmured with a swat to Jasper's ass.

Jasper grinned and filled his plate, and Vincent was glad to see it was more than he'd been eating the last couple of days.

Once he had his own plate and had settled at the table, he eyed Jasper. "Where's your head at today?"

Jasper shot him a curious look. "I'm okay… I'm up for anything."

Vincent hesitated, then remembered how Jasper had circled the slave for a day option. "If you still want to give up making decisions, I can make you my slave for the day."

"Yes," Jasper said, heat staining his cheeks as he straightened. "Please."

"Do you still want to stop using condoms?"

Jasper's flush darkened as he flicked his tongue against his lips. "Yes."

Vincent let out a satisfied hum and motioned for Jasper to finish eating. If Jasper wanted to forget the past few days, he could help with that. It might not be the healthiest response, but Vincent was of the opinion that Jasper's father had earned the contempt of his sons. There wasn't anything for Jasper to do from here, and it was clear he hadn't been wanted or needed there by anyone but Amber. The least Vincent could do was help him enjoy himself for the rest of their time here.

Once they finished eating, he left Jasper to clean up as he retrieved a blindfold and two pairs of cuffs from the playroom, then motioned Jasper upstairs to the bathroom. "For the next few hours, you're completely mine," he said, turning Jasper to face him. "Give me control. You don't need to worry about anything except your safeword or the signals I request of you."

Jasper's throat worked as he swallowed. "Yes, Sir," he whispered. "I'm all yours."

"Good boy." Vincent pulled him in for slow lingering kisses while divesting him of what little clothing he had on. Then he pointed out the hand grips near the top of the shower. "Hold on to those."

Jasper stepped into the stall and grabbed on to them, adjusting his hands before glancing over his shoulder.

"Good." Vincent lifted the blindfold and waited for Jasper's nod to secure it around his eyes. He rested his hands on Jasper's shoulders and brushed a kiss against his ear. "Relax, pet. I'll take good care of you."

Jasper tilted his head enough that Vincent caught the faint smile on his lips. "You always do, Sir."

He squeezed Jasper's shoulders, then turned the water on and let it warm up while he stripped and stepped into the stall. Once the water changed from frigid to warm he switched it to come out of the detachable showerhead, then turned his attention to soaking every inch of Jasper below his neck. He used his free hand to guide the water and chase the goose bumps rippling across Jasper's back. On the second pass, Jasper tipped forward as some of the tension finally eased out of his shoulders.

"Good boy." He put the showerhead back in its place and angled the water to hit their chests, then grabbed the cloth to soap it up. "We'll have Ash take photos the day after tomorrow," he murmured as he dragged the cloth across Jasper's shoulders. He kept his movements slow and firm, massaging as much as scrubbing. "Then have lunch with them the day after."

Jasper let out a long breath and relaxed further. "Yes, Sir."

"For now, I'm going to explore your body in ways I haven't been able to yet." Jasper's quiet moan was all eager anticipation, and Vincent couldn't resist pressing his lips to Jasper's ear. "Starting with tasting every inch of you."

Jasper whimpered and rocked his hips back, but Vincent shifted aside before he could make contact.

"Patience," he said, then set out to test Jasper's patience as he resumed washing. One hand scrubbed while the other caressed, massaged, or stroked by turns. As he worked his way down Jasper's body, he made sure to find and exploit every sensitive point he'd learned of over the past few months. Jasper's neck and nipples were a given, but there was also the spot behind his ear, the one below his ribs, and the inside of his left thigh up to his hip.

When he reached Jasper's groin he spent a long few minutes ensuring he was thoroughly cleaned, his own cock taking interest in the promise of finally getting his mouth on Jasper. By the time he finished actually washing them both and grabbed the showerhead for a rinse, Jasper's breathing had deepened, and he'd pressed his forehead to the wall for balance.

Vincent settled his palm against Jasper's back as he shut off the water, then snagged a towel. He wiped himself dry with a few brisk passes and wrapped the towel around his waist. With a second towel in hand he turned back to Jasper and dried him with the same meticulous attention as he had with washing. When he was satisfied, he helped Jasper out of the shower without removing the blindfold and guided him to the bed.

"Lie back," he murmured, grabbing the lube as Jasper stretched out on the bed. As much as he liked restraints in general, he left Jasper's hands free and settled on the bed next to him. The lube he tossed next to the pillow before leaning over and kissing Jasper's neck. "Comfortable?" he asked softly.

"Uh-huh."

"Good." He breathed in the clean scent of skin as he leisurely kissed and nibbled his way down and across Jasper's chest. "You don't need permission to come today. The only rule is that you tell me when you're getting close," he said, pausing at a nipple to tease it into a hard nub with his teeth.

Jasper arched beneath him with a moan, his hand lifting from the bed as if to grab on to Vincent before he forced it back down.

"Understand?"

He swallowed twice before he found his voice. "Yes, Sir."

"Good boy." He grasped Jasper's hand and brought it to his lips, flicking his tongue against his wrist before guiding Jasper's fingers into his hair. They were both going to enjoy this. There'd be plenty of time to torture Jasper by restraining him and edging him with a blow job some other time. For now he wanted Jasper uninhibited and mindless with pleasure.

He closed his eyes for a moment when Jasper's fingers curled in a loose grip in his hair, then got back to the task at hand by tormenting both nipples. Once they were hard and pinked, he continued down past Jasper's stomach. Something dangerously close to excitement fluttered in his gut as he moved lower. He'd wanted to taste Jasper since they'd signed their first contract.

The last man he'd properly had his mouth on was Adam, who indulged in enough wine and whiskey and the occasional expensive cigar that giving him a blow job had never been as pleasant as it could have been. But Vincent enjoyed the act itself too much to give it up entirely. Some in the community thought a Dom should never be on his knees, but Vincent would never deny his own pleasures to cater to asinine opinions.

He slipped a hand between Jasper's legs and pressed his fingers into a thigh, his mouth nearing Jasper's cock and hovering there with his lips barely touching it. Above him Jasper sucked in a sharp breath, his fingers flexing tighter in Vincent's hair, a tremor running through his body as he aborted an instinctive thrust.

Vincent settled himself against Jasper's leg and slid his hand to the opposite hip, then finally gave in to temptation and dragged his tongue along the underside of Jasper's cock.

Jasper's moan was lost beneath the sudden white noise rushing through Vincent. Nothing else mattered except for the sharp bite of fingers fisting his hair, the warm flesh beneath his palms, the lingering scent of soap on clean skin, and the salty tang of the first drops of Jasper's precum. He lost all sense of time as he slowly, methodically traced his tongue over every centimeter of Jasper's growing erection.

Only when he'd worked his way from base to tip and back again twice did he finally take the head into his mouth. He held it there, closing his eyes as he teased the head and slit with the tip of his tongue.

"Fuck. I'm close. I'm close!"

It took every ounce of willpower to pull his mouth off Jasper before he came, but he managed. If only with a bit of help from Jasper's insistent tugging on his hair. He dropped his forehead to Jasper's stomach and waited for him to catch his breath, his thumbs rubbing soothing circles into Jasper's hips.

"Good?" he asked after a long moment. His voice was already rough, and he hadn't even gotten to the good parts yet.

"Uh-huh."

He didn't waste time with more teasing. He wanted to feel the full weight and length of Jasper's cock on his tongue and took him into his mouth until he felt pressure against the back of his throat.

Jasper bucked beneath him with a shout, and Vincent hummed around him until he made a strangled gurgling sound. He moved his hand to the base of Jasper's cock and wrapped his fingers tight around it. He had no intention of letting Jasper come so soon, but he also wasn't going to pull off again until he was satisfied. He had a feeling that meant Jasper would be getting off sooner than he liked, so it was a good thing Jasper was still young enough to have a shorter refractory period.

He swallowed and flexed his tongue, relishing the noises Jasper made. The way his thighs and stomach tensed as he fought the instinct to push deeper into Vincent's throat. He settled more of his weight across Jasper's legs and worked him over like he'd wanted to do for months. He circled his tongue around the entire length and massaged Jasper's balls with his palm as he tightened and loosened his grip in a slow rhythm.

He cataloged every change in Jasper's skin with his tongue. The lines of his veins and the dips and curves of his flesh. The salty tang of him grew stronger every minute, and Vincent knew neither of them would last much longer. As much as he wanted to draw this out, he wanted to taste Jasper more, and getting the first orgasm out of the way would make it easier to indulge in the next steps.

Jasper jerked beneath him with a gasping moan, and Vincent paused before carefully repeating his last movements. He swallowed as he slowly dragged his lips up until the head of Jasper's cock popped out of his throat, and Jasper keened. With a soft growl Vincent settled into the new rhythm as he did that over and over again, until Jasper's panting turned labored and his limbs moved in a constant restless desperation.

"Please," he sobbed, and Vincent relented, relaxing his tight grip and rubbing a fingertip against Jasper's entrance instead. "Close!" Jasper shouted, barely getting the word out completely before he came.

Vincent swallowed and swallowed again until Jasper went limp, his chest heaving and fingers twitching as they slipped free of Vincent's hair. He hummed at the sensation of Jasper softening in his mouth, then finally pulled away.

He crawled up Jasper's body to stretch out partially on top of him, tucking a leg between Jasper's so his thigh was pressed against Jasper's groin. When he was settled, he tipped Jasper's head back and kissed him. Long, deep kisses that kept Jasper breathless until he found his second wind.

Eventually even Vincent's patience ran thin, and he pulled back. "Not done with you yet, pet," he murmured, sliding off the bed long enough to get situated between Jasper's legs.

Jasper barely needed any coaxing to pull his knees up, and Vincent dug his fingers into the offered ass, spreading him open and focusing on his hole with a soft growl. He dragged his thumb against it, enjoying the way it twitched and Jasper's pleading moan. When he leaned down and exhaled against the same spot, Jasper sputtered.

"What are you—"

Vincent didn't let him finish, cutting off his question as he licked Jasper from hole to balls.

"Fuck!" Jasper yelled, twisting and slamming his thighs shut against Vincent's head.

Undeterred, Vincent returned to Jasper's entrance and began working him open, starting with licking slow circles that grew ever smaller until he wiggled the tip of his tongue past the tight muscle. Jasper's curses grew louder before devolving into groans, both his hands fisted in Vincent's hair and doing his best to pop Vincent's head off with his thighs.

Only Vincent's grip on Jasper's ass saved him from suffocating. Maybe he should have restrained him after all, but it was too late to worry about that. He was far more interested in getting his tongue inside his squirming brat.

He sank his teeth into Jasper's ass in warning, stifling his chuckle when Jasper yelped, but when he pressed his tongue in again and Jasper continued thrashing, he pushed Jasper's hip up and over until he twisted onto his stomach. Then he pinned Jasper's legs down, spread his ass, and attacked with lips and teeth and tongue. Mostly tongue. Circling and licking, delving and probing. By the time he worked it halfway in, Jasper was grinding against the mattress with sharp choked-off moans.

Vincent groaned and dug his fingers harder into Jasper's flesh, spreading him wider; his sole purpose for existing narrowed to giving Jasper the best rim job he'd ever had, even if it was likely his first. He didn't hold back, making sure to give his balls and cock ample attention while he was at it.

He wasn't sure how long it was, minutes or over an hour, before Jasper found a way onto his knees and rocked back into Vincent's ministrations. Soft pleas interspersed between groans that grew louder by the second. "Close," Jasper gasped. "Close, close, close."

Vincent reluctantly pulled away and reached for the lube, sliding his other hand up Jasper's back. "Condom?" he asked. He doubted Jasper was in any state to make a coherent decision, but he had to offer one last time to be sure.

"No way," Jasper growled, turning his head as if trying to glare at him through the blindfold and his sweat-soaked bangs. "Wanna feel you."

Vincent hummed his approval and coated two fingers to press into Jasper. That was all the prep he bothered with. He added more lube to his aching cock, then gripped Jasper's hips and eased himself inside. He managed a quiet, gritted out "Fuck" as he sank into Jasper. His vision nearly whited out with the pleasure of having nothing between them.

When Jasper arched beneath him, he wrapped an arm around Jasper's chest, bracing his other hand against the mattress and pressing his face against Jasper's neck. He breathed in the scent of clean sweat and the musk of sex as he focused on the tight heat wrapped around him. He tried to hold still, wanting to savor the sensation as long as possible, but he'd held back enough already.

He sealed his lips against Jasper's pulse point, unable to resist biting into flesh as he began thrusting.

Jasper keened and moved to meet his thrusts, and for too brief a time the only sounds were flesh meeting flesh, ragged breaths, and their sounds of pleasure.

Vincent didn't last nearly as long as he would have liked. All too soon his orgasm overwhelmed him. He pinned Jasper to the bed as he came, stifling his soft guttural moans in blond hair.

Jasper squirmed beneath him, fighting against his hold. "Sirrr," he whined.

He briefly considered leaving Jasper hard and desperate, but he knew he wouldn't be getting it up again. At least not quickly enough for the torment not to turn to torture. He slid a hand from Jasper's hip, reached beneath him, and gripped his cock before stroking at an unrelenting pace. He dragged his tongue along the shell of Jasper's ear, then bit down with a growled, "Come."

Jasper didn't disappoint. His scream was muffled against the pillow, but his body shuddered and tightened almost painfully around Vincent's softening cock.

They collapsed to the bed, and Vincent shifted enough to pull out and not squish Jasper. With a groan he snagged his towel to wipe them down, then removed the blindfold to toss aside. "Good?" he asked, running his fingers through damp hair. His only answer was an unintelligible gurgle before Jasper rolled closer and wrapped himself around Vincent. Two heartbeats later he was snoring.

Vincent snorted quietly and pulled the covers over them with a yawn. "I'll take that as a yes."

Chapter 20

Why he'd agreed to a dawn photo shoot, Vincent wasn't sure. The only thing worse than being up at sunrise from an inability to sleep through the night was his alarm going off while it was still dark outside. He smacked said phone with a grumbled curse until it finally shut up and promptly shoved his face into his pillow.

Jasper stirred behind him and rolled closer to plaster himself against Vincent with a sleepy mumble.

"Need to get up," Vincent murmured, smiling faintly at the long whine of protest that earned. He blew out a breath and pulled the pillow off his face to smack Jasper with. "Up," he ordered and desperately wished he could ignore the order himself.

Jasper bit his shoulder with a growl before rolling away as it devolved into another whine. "Why did I agree to this?"

Vincent didn't bother answering. He was tired enough he'd likely say something foolish like *Because you love me*. It was too early to think they were feeling anything but lust for each other despite their chemistry both in and out of bed. Another month or two and maybe he could believe it was something more.

When he heard the shower turn on, he finally stopped stalling and tossed the covers off. He used the bathroom, then headed down to rummage through the playroom. He already had an idea of how he wanted Jasper for the photos, but he picked through the toys and accessories to see what he could add.

Silver nipple clamps with a short, thin chain and rods of Asclepius dangling on the ends caught his eye. Leave it to Zach to have pieces to fit all the themes in the room. He picked them up and continued on, though nothing else called out to him before he reached the bundles of Shibari rope. This time he picked only the black, since most of the photos he wanted were going to be black and white anyway.

He paused by the stash of collars on his way out and hooked his fingers around a simple black leather one. He'd yet to put one on Jasper and knew the moment he did that he'd want to keep it there, but that was a risk worth taking. What was the point of having professional photos taken if his sub didn't look the part as much as possible?

He snatched the collar, headed back upstairs to dump his haul on the bed, then took a quick shower while Jasper was making a light breakfast. Once he was dressed in jeans and a T-shirt he joined Jasper at the table and pressed a kiss to the top of his head. It was still too early for him to be hungry, but he managed to eat most of a piece of toast before his stomach threatened to revolt.

Jasper only ate a few bites before giving up, and Vincent wondered if maybe he should have fought Ash a bit harder on the scheduling, but they were already up. They could sleep after.

He ushered Jasper up to the loft and found a pair of tight black boxers for him.

"Is this all I'm going to wear?"

"Technically, no," Vincent answered, unwinding the black rope.

Jasper grumbled something under his breath that sounded like "Such a dick."

"I could leave you naked, if you like," he said and pretended not to see the narrow-eyed glare Jasper shot him. "Or maybe you'd prefer nothing but a cock ring."

"You made your point, Sir," Jasper groused.

"Have I?" he asked, looping the rope around Jasper's back like a lasso and pulling him closer. "I have other suggestions." He snickered when Jasper rolled his eyes, adjusting the rope so the center was resting against the back of Jasper's neck. Then he set to work on an elaborate harness.

The familiar motions and texture as the rope slid between his fingers were soothing, more so when he got them right the first time and didn't feel the need to undo and rework his knots to keep them tight and neat. Jasper's breathing slowed and deepened as Vincent worked, and he glanced up to find Jasper's eyes half lidded. "Don't fall asleep."

He heaved a sigh and audibly forced back a whine even as he swayed on his feet. "So tired."

"Maybe you should stop staying up so late," Vincent taunted, smirking in the face of Jasper's accusing glare and baleful grumble. "Should I add letting you get your beauty sleep to the contract?"

"Yes. Otherwise I might bite you even more."

Vincent hummed in amusement and tied off the rope as he reached the end of it, then stepped back to check over his work. Rather than the typical diamonds, he'd covered Jasper's torso with a line down the center that had acute angles coming off to wrap around his sides and back. They overlapped in different directions for an abstract pattern that drew the attention in and down.

He debated a moment on continuing the pattern down Jasper's legs, but a knock at the patio door let him know they were out of time. He motioned Jasper to get the robe hanging on the bathroom door as he pocketed the clamps and collar, then picked up the other bundles of black rope in case he found a nice tree to tie Jasper to. The white blindfold from the other night was on the nightstand, and he grabbed that too before heading downstairs.

Ash was leaning back against the patio railing, camera bag slung across his chest, a small battery-powered lantern in one hand and a travel mug in the other, which he lifted in response to Vincent's quiet "Morning." He glanced to Jasper with a nod, then turned to lead the way onto one of the paths. Vincent reached for Jasper's hand and followed.

They headed towards the hot springs but turned off before reaching them. It was still dark enough to need the lantern, but the sky was starting to gray, and the warm summer night air promised a hotter day to follow. After a few more minutes of walking on a path Vincent could barely recognize as a path, they reached a small clearing.

Ash stopped a few steps in and turned. "Will this work?"

Vincent couldn't see much other than a tree near the center, but he trusted Ash to know the best spots for photos, especially around his own home. "Yes."

Ash set the lantern on the ground, followed by his mug and bag. "We'll only have an hour or so," he said quietly.

Vincent only knew about the golden hour from listening to Ash in college. He didn't speak much, but photography was his passion, and Zach could always wheedle more than a few sentences out of him by asking about his cameras or photography. Vincent supposed being raised in a cult, as Ash had been, would leave its mark on anyone.

He left Ash to get set up and turned to Jasper. "Ready?"

"Not really," Jasper murmured, his arms wrapped tight around himself.

Vincent considered him for a moment, then grasped his chin to tip his head up. "You can still say no, pet."

Jasper's shoulders relaxed, and his lips twitched in a faint smile. "I know, but I didn't know I was going to be naked *outside*."

"You're not naked," he replied, resisting the powerful urge to roll his eyes. He could have suggested Jasper be naked—Ash did full-nudity photos—but he didn't need something that explicit. At least not for Jasper's first time.

He tugged on the robe, and Jasper heaved a put-upon sigh before letting it slip open and off. Vincent pulled the clamps out and dangled them in front of Jasper as he circled the thumb of his other hand around an exposed nipple.

Jasper shivered as it hardened and let out a soft, sweet moan when the metal bit into it. Once the other was in place Vincent gave them a flick, then turned to take in the clearing. As the sun finally peeked over the horizon, golden streaks of light filtered through the trees to highlight a weeping willow tree standing off-center, its long tendrils hanging in a picturesque canopy. One section had been pruned back to create an opening near one of the sturdy low-hanging branches, leaving a cascading curtain around the space.

He unspooled the extra rope as he moved towards the branch, sure Ash and Zach had set this area up specifically for a kinky photo shoot option for their guests. He tossed the rope over the branch in a simple slipknot, then turned to motion Jasper over. With the other bundle, he created two loops around Jasper's right leg and ran the excess rope up his back, where he left enough length to secure Jasper's right wrist against his lower back.

He worked as quickly as he could, aware of Ash lingering near his bag and trying to appear busy, but he only ever needed a minute or two to get ready. When Vincent finally finished, Jasper's right leg and left arm were attached to the branch above their heads, and his right wrist was restrained behind him. It left him balanced on one foot, his body stretched up and on helpless display.

With the soft sunlight filtering into the clearing, he looked… "Stunning," Vincent murmured. He stepped behind Jasper and ducked his head to press a kiss to his neck as he pulled out the collar and fastened it into place.

Jasper tipped his head back with an audible gasp that nearly masked the sound of the camera shutter.

Vincent stood with one hand on Jasper's stomach, the other settling possessively against his throat and the simple leather collar. "Good?" he murmured, dragging his nose up the side of Jasper's throat. He smelled good. Not that he ever smelled bad. Maybe it was the summer breeze or the thick scent of green growing things around them that enhanced his scent, but Vincent found it addicting at the moment.

More likely it was the fact Jasper was tied up and allowing Ash to take photos simply because Vincent asked. No begging or negotiating or compromise. No promising something of greater value in return. He could have offered Adam a weeklong vacation to Paris and still not gotten an agreement for something like this.

"Thank you, pet," he murmured, lightly dragging his teeth against Jasper's earlobe. He pressed closer when Jasper shivered, his weight slumping into Vincent as if his leg threatened to give out.

Jasper turned his head to bump his nose against Vincent's chin. "For what?"

For what, indeed. For being a reasonable person who didn't view a relationship as a give and take where each person only played one role? For being willing to try new things? For being honest?

"For being you."

Jasper blinked, a soft smile touching his lips. "You make it easy."

Vincent didn't recognize the quiet noise he made, or the sudden tight warmth in his chest, but he knew it wasn't bad. That it might have even been close to what he'd been searching for all these years, even if he wouldn't jinx it by giving it a name.

He became hyperaware of Ash and his camera and the steady click of the shutter. He was almost afraid to see the photos tomorrow and find that unnameable thing staring back at him. He lifted his head and slid his hand from Jasper's throat, letting his fingers trail down and across Jasper's chest instead. "Ready?"

Jasper raised an eyebrow. "I thought we already started."

Vincent smirked and pulled the blindfold from his pocket, and Jasper tipped his head back with a dramatic groan. "Fiiine."

CHAPTER 21

JASPER SIGHED as Vincent pulled away the last of the Shibari rope, lightly dragging his fingers over the indents left behind in his skin. He swayed forward when Vincent's fingers trailed behind his own, letting his head drop against Vincent's shoulder. The photo shoot hadn't been particularly strenuous, and they didn't even have sex after, but his head was pleasantly fuzzy, and his limbs were nearly too heavy to lift. It was a sensation he enjoyed, especially since it usually meant Vincent had properly used him. Apparently that didn't have to mean sex.

He nuzzled against Vincent's throat and breathed in the lingering scent of summer heat and moss. When Vincent tugged him towards the shower, he followed, but he was of absolutely no help when it came to getting the smudges of dirt and bright green stains off. The warm water was heaven on his skin, and he closed his eyes, tipping his head back as it rained down over his face.

The slick-rough touch of a cloth on his back drew a long, deep groan out of him. "So good." He really could get used to this; letting Vincent take care of him. It was almost as addictive as the sex, and the kink, and the heated looks that made him want *more*. So, so much more.

A light smack to his ass startled him out of the blissful doze he'd fallen into, and he turned enough to see Vincent eyeing him with amusement. "You can go back to bed now," he said, groping Jasper's ass before pushing the curtain open enough to let him out.

Jasper leaned in to steal a kiss first, then snagged a towel to scrub himself dry. He pulled on a pair of boxers and flopped onto the bed, rubbing the fading rope impressions on his wrists with a happy sigh. As much as he wanted to go back to sleep, he was more awake now, so he retrieved his handheld from the drawer of the nightstand and stretched out to continue his game.

He was so invested in the cutscene of the hot red-eyed blond guy betraying the group to save his reincarnated husband that he didn't even notice Vincent joining him until a warm hand slid across his chest. He squeaked in surprise and reflexively tried to hide the game by rolling over, which only served to put his face in Vincent's chest.

"What are you playing?"

Jasper swallowed a whine and bit his tongue against saying *Nothing*. "A game."

"You don't say." Vincent snorted softly and tangled his fingers in Jasper's hair. "Is it hentai?"

He narrowed his eyes and tilted his head enough to bite Vincent's wrist. "No."

"Pity."

Jasper huffed and wiggled closer to tuck himself bodily against Vincent. "It's a sci-fi male otome game," he murmured, waiting for the condescending mockery he usually got for his game choices. But none came.

Vincent only asked, "Which one is your favorite?" He settled his hand on Jasper's hip and settled a leg over top of Jasper's. "Hmm?" he prompted when Jasper didn't answer, nibbling on his earlobe.

No way could he answer that. He might have been obsessed with the red-eyed blond when he first started playing, but that was before the dark-haired, moody Cyprus, who kept trying to seduce the MC with promises of bringing his fantasies to life, was introduced.

"Are you not going to tell me?"

Jasper wriggled back enough to roll over and crawl away, though he didn't get far before Vincent dragged him back. "Noooo. You can't make me." He turned the game off and shoved it to the other side of the bed.

Vincent swatted Jasper's ass. "Fine, be a brat." He stretched out over Jasper to pin him to the bed. "We have a few days left. How do you want to spend them?"

Jasper grunted as he rolled onto his back to get his arms around Vincent's neck. "I still want to try that ziplining thing." Vincent tried to hide his grimace, but Jasper noticed anyway and grinned. "Are you scared of heights, Sir?"

"I'm not fond of them, no," he replied dryly.

Jasper shrugged. "We still have the hot springs."

"Do you want to go tonight?"

He tipped his head back and forth as he considered but then shook his head no. It was early enough they could go find something to do, but he was still exhausted from the trip back home and getting up too early. Plus he needed to be rested to enjoy seeing Zach and Ash again tomorrow. "Movie?"

"Sounds good."

BY THE next morning the haze had worn off, and Jasper was finally feeling more like himself. He hadn't dared turn his phone on since the plane landed and was sure he had dozens of missed calls or texts, but Amber hadn't tried to contact him through Vincent, so he assumed his father was still alive. That or Amber had finally gotten the hint and knew not to bother him either way until he was back home for good.

He shoved thoughts of family out of his mind and focused on the day ahead. Vincent was taking him zip lining before spending the rest of the day with Zach and Ash. He bounced lightly in his seat after he buckled, excited to be getting away from the cabin and doing something not kink related.

And that was a thought he never expected to have. He loved exploring kinks and having sex, but he was a bit relieved that the obsessive novelty of enjoying something new was fading. Not that he'd ever admit it, and he really hoped that didn't mean he'd get bored with kink. The last thing he wanted was to lose the biggest thing they had in common. He doubted even Vincent would keep their contract if Jasper lost interest in being a sub.

"What's wrong?" Vincent asked.

Jasper blinked innocent eyes at him. "What?"

Vincent flicked his fingers at Jasper's leg where it was bouncing as if he'd downed a gallon of coffee. "Are you nervous?"

"It's not that," Jasper said, then silently cursed himself for not taking the obvious out. "It's just… nice to get out of the cabin."

Vincent hummed, and Jasper felt a heavy stare on him before he turned back to the road. "Should we have dinner somewhere?"

"No," Jasper said quickly. "I like your cooking. Unless you don't want to make dinner?" He'd volunteer, but he'd only learned to make a few dishes, and they never turned out as good as when Vincent made them.

"I don't mind cooking."

Jasper nodded, hating the sudden nervous energy buzzing through him. He had no reason to be nervous. It was normal to stop being obsessed with things. Right? That didn't mean he enjoyed it any less. Vincent had been involved with kink for years and even owned a club dedicated to it, so Jasper shouldn't worry.

This wasn't like a new hobby or game that he'd shelve in a few weeks or months. This was an integral part of who he was and wanted to be. He'd never felt more alive and like himself than he had the past few months.

He loved being with Vincent. Loved being at the club and seeing how many others shared the same interest as him. No way would he ever get bored of that. The only way he'd leave was if Vincent made him, but Jasper couldn't see that happening no matter how much he feared it might. Even if they broke up, Vincent wouldn't ban him from the club. Being able to afford a membership was another issue entirely.

"Are you paying for my club membership?"

Vincent let out a startled huff of laughter. "Technically your fees have been waived as you're marked as my sub. Why?"

Jasper shrugged. "Just curious," he murmured. Not like he could admit to wondering what would happen if they broke up. He doubted he'd even want to be in the same club as Vincent if they did, and he needed to stop thinking about it before he psyched himself out. They had a contract for a year. He didn't need to worry about keeping Vincent's attention until that time got close to ending.

The drive to the zip-line area was relatively short, and Vincent parked in a shaded area near the entrance. There were signs inside the small building advertising a rock-climbing space and the lake, but they paid the entrance fee, signed waivers, and followed the arrows for the zip lines to a tall wooden, tower-like structure.

A guide stopped them at the bottom to get them geared up. Jasper hooked his fingers in the straps with a grin, the new flutter in his stomach more excitement than worry. He never got to try new things like this. Part of him was full of guilt that he was using Vincent's money for outlandish activities that Vincent didn't even want to do, but the rest was completely on board with indulging for his birthday.

It wasn't until they were heading up the tower that he noticed Vincent trailing behind. He stopped and stepped to the side to wait, bouncing lightly on the balls of his feet. "Too much exercise for your decrepit body, Sir?" he asked, not at all dissuaded by the dark glower Vincent shot him over the top of his sunglasses.

"Watch it, or I'll throw you off the top," he threatened as he continued by.

Jasper gasped. "You're going to *murder* me? What did I ever do to you? Except let you molest me and do vile, depraved, unspeakable things to me!"

"What did I do that was unspeakable?"

Jasper let out another more exaggerated gasp. "You pretended to be a doctor and beeped my beepin' beep beep and beepity beep," he stage-whispered, somehow managing to keep a straight face and sound scandalized while making terrible censor sounds.

Vincent glanced over his shoulder. "And if you keep this up, I'll beep your beep with a beeping beep."

Jasper cackled, closed the distance between them with a few quick steps, and groped Vincent's ass twice, once with each hand in rapid succession, with a "Beep beep!" Then he hurried past and up the rest of the stairs, where he waited with as much patience as he could for Vincent to catch up. Only when they neared the launch point did he notice Vincent was paler than usual, and he kept flexing his fingers while keeping his other hand on the nearest railing or support.

Oh.

"Wait, are you really scared of heights?" Fuck, he was so stupid. Vincent had been anything but enthusiastic about coming here. "We don't have to do this."

"A bit late now," Vincent replied tightly, looking anywhere but at the edge and the sharp drop.

"We can go back down the stairs."

"No." Vincent curled his fingers into a tight, bloodless fist.

"Next!" the operator called.

Jasper glanced over to find they were the only ones left in line, but the operator could wait. He reached for Vincent's hand and forced his fingers open and apart until he could get his own between them. "I don't want to do it that badly. You should have said you didn't want to."

Vincent's fingers went lax for a moment before he squeezed them around Jasper's. "It was the only thing you asked for."

Jasper's chest turned squishy, and he bit his tongue before he could call Vincent an idiot. "Doesn't mean you should have agreed," he said instead. "Aren't you supposed to be setting an example? What if this was some kink you didn't want to do?"

Vincent narrowed his eyes but notably didn't have an immediate response. "Then I'd be an adult and weigh the gains against the risks before making a decision. Same as I did before bringing you here. Now let's go."

He huffed and turned for the platform without letting go of Vincent's hand. His stomach swooped as he stopped by the operator and saw how far down the ground was. Maybe he should have picked something else after all. He would have probably died trying to climb a rock wall, but surely there was some activity around here that didn't involve risking life or limb.

"You gentlemen ready?" the operator asked, offering them a bright smile as she waved a metal hook at them, which likely wasn't meant to look as threatening as it did.

"Nope!" Jasper squeezed Vincent's fingers tight enough he probably cut off their blood supply. "Can we go together?"

"Sure." She motioned them closer to the line stretching out across the trees. The end wasn't in sight, but that was the least of his worries. More concerning was the faint tremor in Vincent's hand.

The operator was speaking, but between the nervous excitement clawing through Jasper's gut and the tingling sensation forming in his fingers, everything else was a rush of white noise. He blinked and they were hooked to the line, Vincent standing behind him with an arm wrapped around Jasper's chest, the trees stretched out below and around them.

"Step off when you're ready."

He was going to be sick.

"Pet," Vincent murmured, close enough his lips brushed Jasper's ear.

He leaned back with a shiver and sucked in a deep breath that was still too shallow. "Ready," he lied, gripping Vincent's hand on his chest.

Vincent's fingers twitched tighter in Jasper's shirt before he tipped ever so slightly forward.

Jasper's lungs seized as his feet hit empty air, and he clawed at Vincent's hand as the trees rushed past and the ground came closer. His stomach somersaulted, his lungs unfroze, and he screamed. He kept screaming until he had to take a breath, and then he started laughing as the shock gave way to exhilaration, and he realized they weren't moving as fast as it felt.

They were still dangling a few stories off the ground, but the gear felt solid around his body. Part of him was sure they would fall at any moment, but that was part of the thrill—the same uncertain swoop of excitement as when Vincent restrained or blindfolded him.

He squeezed Vincent's hand with a delighted laugh, releasing the death grip of his other hand on his harness and stretching his arm out. He was flying, or at least as close as he'd ever get. The trees racing past, the warm wind on his face, Vincent's solid, sturdy body against his back. He wouldn't mind if it took hours to get to the end.

All too soon the landing area came into view, and they slowed to a stop. He stumbled forward once they were free and steadied himself against the nearest wall, a giddy lightness making his legs shaky. "That was fun. Wanna go again?" he asked, grinning when Vincent eyed him in dismay. "Wasn't there another one that starts even higher?" When that earned a grimace, he pushed off the wall and propped himself against Vincent's chest instead. "Or you can wait here while I go again."

Vincent grunted softly and hooked an arm around his waist. "No," he murmured.

"Gonna come with me, then?"

"No."

Jasper snorted and looped his arms around Vincent's neck before nuzzling into it. "Come on, it wasn't that bad, was it?"

"Worst thing I've done this year."

Jasper rolled his eyes and wiggled his fingers into Vincent's hair, but he couldn't deny it was almost a relief to see at least something could get under Vincent's skin. It made him seem more human instead of a perfect sex god, though in a different way from his needing reading glasses.

"I'm going again," he said, kissing the tip of Vincent's nose before twisting away despite the tightening arms attempting to keep hold of him.

The second time was as exhilarating as the first even if the lack of Vincent against his back was a disappointment, but he did manage to coax Vincent into joining him on the third run, even if Vincent looked like he was going to pass out on the climb up the stairs.

By the time he'd gone another two times, it was afternoon, and he was getting hungry, so they headed back to the cabins to have lunch with Zach and Ash.

Jasper was a strange mess of anxious excitement and exhaustion from the adrenaline crash, which was probably why he stared at Vincent with a pout when he headed downstairs with Ash to go through the pictures from the photo shoot. The only bright side was when Zach tugged him into the living room to play video games.

CHAPTER 22

VINCENT BREATHED a sigh of relief as the basement wrapped its cool, dim arms around him. He hadn't realized how overstimulated he'd gotten from the zip lines until the silence seeped into him. He didn't regret it. He couldn't. Not when Jasper had enjoyed himself so thoroughly, but he was exhausted in a way reminiscent of his weeks of physical therapy while adjusting to living in a new country.

Tension slowly leaked out of his limbs and neck as he took several deep breaths, then settled in a chair next to Ash at his computer. A folder with Jasper's photos was already on the screen, and Ash opened the first one before rolling his chair aside for Vincent to lean in and take over.

They were gorgeous, which was a given. Even if he was biased, Jasper was striking. More so with the early morning light turning his hair and skin golden. The fact he was bound only added to his appeal. A soft thrum of pleasure suffused his limbs as he clicked through every picture.

A full body shot of Jasper tied to the tree and blindfolded, the light casting teasing shadows across his chest and stomach, his head tilted towards his left arm as though unsure if he should try to hide his face. Close-ups of his face and chest, with Vincent's fingers pressed against his lips from behind. Pressed past his lips. Gripping his chin, slick with a glint of saliva. Jasper's head tipped back, lips parted on a gasp or a moan, Vincent's teeth sinking into his earlobe.

Ash had obviously sorted through the pictures to organize them and show the cleanest ones, because even some of Jasper's impromptu pictures in the basement were scattered through. A dozen clicks later Vincent found the one from the conversation before he'd put the blindfold on. His finger froze on the button as he stared, his breath sticking in his throat. He'd been worried about seeing his own expression, and it was as concerning as he expected, but he was captivated by Jasper's face and the matching expression there.

Ash's voice was quiet when he said, "He's a good sub for you." Vincent dragged his eyes away from the computer to look at him, noting the way his hands were resting in his lap, one hand turning the simple leather bracelet around and around his other wrist, but his shoulders were relaxed, his gaze clear as he studied the picture on the screen before it flicked to meet Vincent's eyes. "You should keep him."

His lips twitched. "That's the plan," he said, surprised by the weight of those words on his tongue. He knew he was getting attached by the simple fact he wanted to collar Jasper, but he hadn't let himself look beyond that. Beyond the end of their current contract. Thinking of "forever" with a young man who was finishing college, who had never lived on his own or even had a driver's license, somehow seemed less of a risk than falling into a relationship with Adam. But then, even that had seemed like the most logical next step at the time.

Years of therapy made it easy to pinpoint the foolish choices in hindsight.

Ash nodded again and reached forward to tap a button to go to the next picture, this one obviously taken in secret. Jasper was free of the ropes and blindfold, his arms thrown around Vincent's neck, a leg hooked against his hip as they kissed. "Maybe you could bring him to visit again."

"Yeah," Vincent agreed, only partially paying attention to the words as he considered the picture. The long line of Jasper's mostly naked body pressed against his own. The possessive grips of his hands on Jasper's hip and hair. When the words finally sank in a moment later he glanced at Ash. "Or you could take your own vacation and come visit."

Ash wrinkled his nose, but without any distaste or fear in his expression. Once Ash got settled somewhere, he usually didn't like to leave. Talking him into coming to the States with Zach had been easy enough, but getting him to leave the little sanctuary they'd built here was basically impossible. Last he'd heard, Ash rarely even left for the kink conventions where Zach sold his BDSM furniture. He'd used to offer photo shoots, though most of their sales were online or through guests staying here these days.

"Maybe," Ash finally murmured, sounding none too happy about it.

"Maybe we could take a trip somewhere. I know you hate being in a city. A beach, maybe."

"We could do that. I've never been."

"I don't think Jasper has either."

"I hear sex on a beach is fun," Ash said, amusement sparking in his eyes.

Vincent snorted. "You'll have to let me know." He preferred to keep his asscrack sand-free as much as possible. He tapped the computer screen. "Can you send this one to my phone? And then I want these in black and white," he said, going back through the photos to point out the ones he liked best. He ordered a few in color for the house, but the others he'd let Jasper pick which ones he'd be willing to put up in the club. He suspected most would end up in his offices, but that was fine too.

JASPER SLUMPED against the sofa with a groan when he died for the fifth time. At Zach's quiet snickering he grabbed the nearest pillow to smack him with. "I don't think this game is for me."

"Aww, giving up already? I didn't take you for a quitter," Zach teased.

"I'm not, I just know what I like." And FPS games definitely weren't it.

"Oh-ho." Zach eyed him with a considering look before grinning. "All right. Let's try something else, then." He rolled to his feet and picked out a different game to pop into the console.

As he was setting up, Jasper idly circled the joystick on his controller with his thumb. "Can I ask…. You don't really seem like a Dom."

Zach laughed. "No, I'm not. I'm mostly a sub, but I get the occasional urge to switch."

Jasper frowned and tilted his head. "What about Ash's collar?"

He hummed and glanced towards the door to the basement with a wry twist of his lips. "That's more of a promise than anything. I'm slightly less subby than Ash, but it helps that I'm imaginative and also know what I like."

He grinned when Jasper eyed him in confusion. "We don't really make sense, but we work. Honestly, for a while in college, I considered asking Vincent to take us both on as his subs, but fuckface kinda fucked that up. And then even after that ended, we were already settled here, and we both prefer this to a city." He raised an eyebrow when Jasper could only stare. "What?"

"Two subs," he said, still stuck on how that could possibly work. The rest of what Zach said went mostly unheard.

Zach smirked. "What, you wouldn't want another sub to play with?"

"No," he said, far too quickly judging by Zach's snicker. The last thing he wanted was to have to share Vincent with someone else. He hardly got enough of him for himself as it was.

Zach started the game, and for a while Jasper was focused on learning the controls. Puzzle games weren't really his thing either, but at least it was better than the chaos of trying to shoot people. But the downside was it wasn't fast-paced enough to keep his mind from wandering.

What if Vincent would prefer another sub? Not like that was something he'd mention. Or would he? That felt like something that would go in a contract. Or was Vincent waiting until the next one to bring something like that up? He hadn't been too forthcoming with things he liked so far, and Jasper hoarded each insight like the precious gems they were. But would Vincent even mention that kind of preference, or would Jasper find out by some throwaway comment in the middle of a scene?

"Uh-oh," Zach murmured. "I know that look."

"What?"

"C'mon, don't fret about it. I'm sure you're more than enough for Master Vincent to handle," he said with a suggestive wiggle of his eyebrows.

Jasper rolled his eyes. "Why do you call him Master Vincent?"

"Mm, 'cause that's the proper way to address him." Zach tilted his head, eyeing Jasper with a sly grin. "You don't call him Master?"

"I have a few times, but usually I call him Sir."

Zach let out a long *hmm* but didn't respond. They fell silent for a while as they played the game, then he asked, "Why don't you call him Master?"

Jasper shrugged, ignoring the heat creeping into his cheeks. "Shouldn't I have a collar for that?" he asked, regretting it the moment he caught Zach's grin in the corner of his eye.

"Do you want a collar?"

Jasper absently touched his throat, but it was nothing like the warm press of Vincent's hand. The nonthreat of pressure that never quite choked or made him gasp for air from more than the thrill. He enjoyed how collars looked and the weight of them. He especially loved when Vincent snagged his tie and pulled it like a leash. "Maybe," he said.

Zach snorted. "Uh-huh."

Jasper huffed and dropped his hand as he turned back to trying to solve the current puzzle. When he finally realized it'd been over an hour, and Vincent and Ash hadn't come back, he started to wonder if maybe Vincent was enjoying being around a sub who actually knew how to be a sub. Ash was quiet, but he seemed nice, so Jasper couldn't really blame him.

Vincent had already given him more than anyone else had in a relationship. He'd never even been on a vacation before now, much less been so well taken care of. And not only sexually. Even cooking or reading or watching TV together was enjoyable.

He ignored the side-eyed glances from Zach as he failed his part of a simple puzzle twice.

By the time Vincent and Ash reappeared, Jasper was ready to go back to their own cabin, though his thoughts kept circling the same black hole. What if being near Zach and Ash reminded Vincent what having a real sub was like? What if he decided Jasper really wasn't worth the effort anymore? What if on top of losing his bastard of a father, he lost Vincent, too, at the end of this?

It wasn't until he finished cleaning up after dinner and Vincent grasped his chin that he realized how much time he'd lost in his own head.

"Not that I don't enjoy the quiet, but what's wrong?"

He blinked at Vincent, opening his mouth on a *Nothing* before snapping it shut. Their contract was for a year. Surely he could trust Vincent to keep him at least that long. But what about after? He'd told himself he didn't need to worry about that yet, but would Vincent be bored of him enough by then to find a new sub? Maybe he'd keep Jasper around while he trained a new sub.

"Do you like Ash?" he finally asked, though it wasn't at all what he wanted to know.

Vincent raised an eyebrow. "I like both Ash and Zach," he said, and Jasper couldn't hide his flinch. He tried to step away, but Vincent caught his wrist in an unrelenting grip. "I thought you liked them? What happened? Did Zach say something?"

He swallowed hard and stared at the lamp across the room. "I did—I do," he said and couldn't say anything else.

Vincent didn't release him, his thumb rubbing a distracting circle against Jasper's inner wrist. He finally sighed and let go, and Jasper barely resisted the need to wrap his own hand around the chill left behind. "Hot springs," Vincent said as he headed upstairs.

Jasper stayed where he was for a long moment, waiting for Vincent to find his swim trunks and a shirt and disappear into the bathroom before trudging up the stairs to change. When Vincent came out, he followed him in silence.

It was dark enough that the few lamps along the path were on, guiding them in small bursts of soft orange light. The only sounds were their footsteps on the gravel, the wind in the leaves, and the droning crickets.

As they neared the hot springs, they crossed paths with another couple, and Jasper nearly tripped as he focused on them. A woman was on her phone, a leash in her other hand that attached to the collar of a man on all fours, naked except for a black leather dog mask and matching tail. On a second glance, Jasper noticed the knee pads, but still couldn't help the internal wince for the man's hands on the pebbled ground. The woman glanced up as they passed and winked at them before turning her attention back to her phone.

He couldn't help glancing behind him after they'd passed, briefly wondering if Vincent wanted him to do something like that, but wearing the fox ears and tail had been enough. Actual petplay didn't seem appealing, and he really hoped that wasn't a kind of role-play Vincent wanted.

The springs were empty when they reached them.

Vincent left his shoes and towel near a bench, the cabin key tossed into a shoe, before he stepped into the water. More lights were hidden in the rocks and bushes around the spring, but the water was dark.

Jasper lingered near the bench and momentarily wondered if snakes liked to hide in hot springs when Vincent sank into the water up to his chest. With a sigh, Jasper kicked off his own shoes near Vincent's, then slipped into the water. It was hot and came up to his shoulders when he slumped onto a rock seat curved from the side. It might have been relaxing if he wasn't so miserably stuck in his own head tonight. He should forget it and be happy with having Vincent all to himself for the rest of their contract, but he couldn't help the niggling worry that Vincent might want to end it early after meeting up with his friends again.

Vincent sighed loudly enough that Jasper knew it was directed at him, and he braced himself for the worst. "I can't fix something if I don't know what's wrong."

"What if it can't be fixed?" Jasper asked, courtesy of the melodramatic voice in his head.

"It certainly won't be if you don't even try," Vincent said tightly before sighing and pinching the bridge of his nose. "Will you come here at least?" he asked after a long moment.

Jasper dug his fingers into the stone beneath him, then slowly waded over to Vincent. He tried to find a place to sit beside him, but Vincent hauled him into his lap and hooked his arms tight around Jasper, like he wouldn't be letting go anytime soon. He let out a harsh breath against Jasper's shoulder. "You're going to have to give me some kind of clue, pet. We're not going back to the cabin until I understand what's going on."

Jasper turned his head away, but he couldn't resist the urge to slump into Vincent's chest for long and soon found himself with his face pressed into Vincent's neck. "Zach said he was going to ask you to be his and Ash's Dom, but douche canoe messed it up."

Vincent was silent for long enough for Jasper to worry that Vincent might be considering taking them up on their offer now, but all he said was "Okay?"

"Is that what you want?" Jasper asked softly.

"Do I want to take on two more subs?" Vincent asked slowly.

Jasper swallowed hard and curled his fingers into the wet cloth of Vincent's shirt. The fact it was soaked and turning near see-through should have been far more distracting than it was, especially when Jasper could see the darker circles of Vincent's nipples, but his attention was on forcing out the words, "Do you want two subs?"

"I'm having enough trouble keeping up with one," he replied dryly, turning his head to press his lips against Jasper's temple. "I have you, so unless you're wanting someone to play with, I'm not following."

"You really wouldn't prefer two subs?"

Vincent sighed and slid a hand along Jasper's leg to hook around his knee. "I can see the appeal of it," he said slowly, "but adding a third to this relationship isn't exactly what it needs right now. Even if I was considering it, I would certainly have a few conversations with you first."

"Or you could tear up the contract and do what you want," Jasper said, the words escaping before he could think to stop them. He knew Vincent wouldn't do that, but knowing didn't help the fear of it.

"Tear up…? Why would I tear up our contract?" Vincent asked, a hard edge to his voice.

"You were going to before," he whispered. He almost thought he'd have to relive those horrible few days again, when he'd made the mistake of pushing Vincent away and lying about being sick, but then Vincent curled his fingers in Jasper's hair and tugged, forcing his head up and back to look at him.

"I said we could void the contract when you lied to me and then refused to explain what was going on," Vincent said, his voice tight. "I am not going to tear up the contract on a whim, and I'm certainly not going to void it because I find someone else attractive. Christ." He swore under his breath, releasing Jasper's hair and tipping his head back as he closed his eyes.

"Sorry," Jasper whispered, tangling his fingers together beneath the water. If not for Vincent's other arm around his lower back he would have crawled away.

"I'm not angry at you, pet," Vincent said before exhaling a long breath. "And thank you for telling me your concerns. For the record, I don't want Ash or Zach as my subs, and I'm not letting you get away so easily."

Jasper stared at the water as his body suddenly became unbearably hot, but Vincent caught his chin tipped it up.

"You are mine," he said, the low, rough edge to his voice sending shivers down Jasper's spine. Goose bumps broke out on his arms despite the heat. "Is that what you needed to hear?"

He stifled a whimper and tried to nod, but Vincent's fingers on his chin forced him to whisper, "Yes, Sir."

"Aside from assuming I would toss you aside or bring someone else into my bed, is there anything else we need to address?" Jasper hesitated a moment too long because Vincent raised an eyebrow. "If I ask Zach what all you talked about, is he going to mention something else?"

Jasper glared. "I don't know. Is he a snitch?"

"If I force his hand he might."

He managed to turn his head enough to bite Vincent's finger. A muffled sound of surprise escaped when Vincent twisted it farther into his mouth to press on his tongue. He latched on to Vincent's arm with both hands but didn't try to pull him away.

Vincent slowly traced his tongue with a fingertip before pulling it out and dragging the wet tip across Jasper's lips. "Are you going to answer me, pet?"

"Collars," he breathed, flicking his tongue against Vincent's finger when it passed over his lips again.

"What about collars?"

"I like them."

Vincent snorted quietly and flicked Jasper's nose. "I'm aware."

Jasper blinked and managed to focus enough to glare at him. "You've never put one on me. A real one, I mean."

Vincent studied him in silence long enough to make him squirm. Finally he said, "Would that be enough to convince you I'm not going to tear up the contract without warning?"

"Maybe," he said softly, though he didn't sound very convincing even to himself.

Vincent settled his hand on Jasper's throat, reducing him to a gasping mess of want with barely any pressure. He let go too quickly and tapped Jasper's thigh. "Is that all?"

Jasper nodded with a faint, "Yes, Sir." He touched his fingers to his throat with a soft sigh and slumped into Vincent. He drifted in a not-quite doze to the burbling of water and a chorus of crickets. Eventually he turned his head to press his face into Vincent's neck. "Sorry," he murmured.

"For what, pet?"

Jasper shrugged. "Being shit at communicating?"

Vincent flexed his fingers against Jasper's hip. "That is definitely something we need to work on."

He lifted his head with a stifled groan, not looking forward to what that meant in the least.

"Ready to head back?"

They hadn't been there long, but the heat was already going to his head. Or maybe that was the effect Vincent had on him. He slid off Vincent's lap and climbed out, shaking water off his arms on the way to his towel. The walk back to the cabin was silent, but when he reached for Vincent's hand, he threaded their fingers together rather than pull away, so Jasper stepped close enough that their arms brushed as they walked. At least if he was going to screw things up every few weeks, Vincent was understanding enough to get them past it. But Jasper was really going to havc to do better if he had any chance of making it to another contract.

CHAPTER 23

VINCENT PICKED through the selection of collars in the playroom with growing dismay. They were all simple, cheap leather or metal. Vincent couldn't exactly expect high quality considering they were free for any guests to use, but if he was going to put a collar on Jasper, he wanted it to be a good one, even if it was temporary.

Maybe he should wait until they were back home. Especially since he had a feeling neither of them would want to remove a collar once it was in place. He wouldn't want Jasper removing it even to go to classes or work, which left most of the leather ones out of the question as too obvious. He'd need a day collar that functioned more like a fashionable necklace.

Giving up on finding a suitable collar here as a lost cause, he headed back upstairs and settled on the bed next to a still-sleeping Jasper. He picked up his phone and waited for it to turn on, then browsed one of his usual stores for kink supplies. They had a decent selection of collars, but none of them called to him. After several minutes of searching in vain, he pulled up one of the specialty sites with a good reputation in the community. Their collar selection was bigger, and he immediately spotted a few that could work, but he didn't want a simple silver band.

Stylish leather didn't feel right either; it needed to have some weight to it. Something Jasper wouldn't be able to ignore easily even when he was used to wearing it.

Jasper stirred beside him, waking enough to roll over and octopus his limbs around Vincent's legs with a sleepy grumble before dozing off again.

Vincent dropped a hand to his head, absently running his fingers through Jasper's hair as he continued browsing. Studs and spikes were out of the question. So were the wide bands with a ring in the center. The ones with a lock were too on the nose even for him.

Finally he found one crafted from woven links of black stainless steel and hovered his thumb over it for a moment before bringing it up. Instead of a single ring in the center it had a double ring. The larger outer ring was a simple solid black circle while the inner ring was interwoven silver like the metal had been twisted around itself until it formed a tight circle. It looked sturdy, and the ring was fashionable while still doubling as a place to hook a leash. Or a finger. There was nowhere to put an engraving, but that was fine. He didn't need to be promising Jasper a forever in so many words. Not until Jasper could trust him not to cancel the contract on a whim, anyway.

He debated only a few moments before adding it to the cart and checking out. He even paid for express delivery to make sure it arrived by the time they returned. Then, while he was apparently in the mood to make potentially life-changing decisions, he made another to offer Jasper a key to his home. It still felt too early, but he suspected it always would.

Adam had been a slow, drawn-out affair through his last years of college. Then they returned to the States and moved in together. Anything was going to seem fast compared to that, and he wasn't too keen on only seeing Jasper a few nights a week for that long. If anything, this vacation had proved they were compatible even with prolonged exposure. Was there really any reason to drag things out longer?

He knew he wanted Jasper. His only worry was that Jasper would realize that any decent Dom would treat him how Vincent was treating him and move on. So far their tastes seemed to align, but the chance Jasper would learn he wanted something Vincent couldn't provide was nonzero. Like whips. He'd had his fill of those. Could barely stand to see them in the club, though at least he didn't flinch at their sharp cracks anymore.

He set his phone aside when he received the order confirmation and turned his attention to Jasper, still dragging his fingers through blond hair. He looked peaceful, though Vincent was fairly sure that was drool he felt seeping into his thigh. "A brat even in your sleep," he murmured, flexing his fingers tighter to elicit a sigh.

Far too easily he could get used to waking up like this on more than just weekends. He hadn't let himself imagine Jasper moving in, knowing his imagination was an idealized, best-case fantasy. Living with Adam had been fine at first. It was only when they'd both settled into their new lives that things started to change for the worse. Things would change with Jasper too, especially once he finished college and started a job. Medical professions, he knew, were rough. Long, demanding hours. Physical labor. The stress of holding literal lives in their hands.

Jasper seemed driven enough to stick with it. Vincent could only hope he wasn't so exhausted at the end of his shifts that he had no time or energy left for Vincent. Not to mention Jasper's tendency to bottle things up rather than talk about them. Sooner or later that could become a much bigger problem, though so far they'd managed to find a way through. Which was far more than he could say about Adam.

He hated comparing Jasper to his ex, but everything about them so far was such a polar opposite that he couldn't help it. Jasper made him feel alive and seen in ways he hadn't felt since his mother was alive. He curled his fingers tighter as he considered that. Was it fear of losing that all over again driving him, or was he overthinking things? He'd been drawn to Jasper from the beginning, on more than a physical attraction level. It wasn't often he found someone he enjoyed being near for an extended period of time, and with Zach and Ash hundreds of miles away, his close circle of friends was basically nonexistent. The only other person he'd consider a close friend was back in London.

With a sigh he shifted down the bed enough to stretch out, careful not to dislodge Jasper as he settled in to try to get more sleep.

He managed to drift off at some point because he was woken by a delicious pressure and heat nuzzling against his groin. He drew in a slow breath and let it out on a soft groan.

Jasper hummed against him, and Vincent rolled to his back with a sigh and propped a knee up to give Jasper more room. He snaked a hand under the covers and tangled his fingers in Jasper's hair.

"Going to do anything but tease, pet?"

"Gettin' to it," Jasper murmured before lightly dragging his teeth over Vincent's sweats and boxers.

Vincent closed his eyes, resisting the urge to pull himself out and push into Jasper's mouth to test his limits. Jasper had initiated this, which was gratifying on its own, and he wanted to see how far his submission would go without Vincent actively guiding him. When Jasper's fingers settled on the waistband of his sweats and then stopped, Vincent gave him a fifty-fifty chance of continuing without some prodding. He held his tongue and waited, silently counting to seventeen before Jasper took a shuddering breath and tugged.

Cool air washed over his hips and groin, but Vincent hardly noticed since he was distracted by the sheer pleasure of Jasper willingly stepping out of his comfort zone. Then hot breath caressed his dick, followed by the hesitant flick of a wet tongue on his bare skin, and he was distracted for an entirely different reason.

He breathed out a groan and flexed his fingers tighter in Jasper's hair before forcing them to release. As much as he wanted to hold Jasper still and take his pleasure, this was nice too. He couldn't remember the last time he'd been woken by a blow job.

Jasper curled a hand against the side of Vincent's cock as he kissed his way down the other side, then licked him from base to tip.

Vincent let out a louder groan as encouragement, relishing the answering shaky breath over his sensitive skin. He let Jasper explore at his own pace, even if it was equal parts torture and bliss. It was so much more intense without a condom between them—not only the wet heat of Jasper's mouth, but the friction of his tongue on skin rather than the vague pressure against rubber. The way Jasper worked his cock in deeper with slow bobs of his head tested Vincent's patience, but he persevered. At least for a while.

When he couldn't remain still any longer, he slid his hand to the back of Jasper's neck and pushed back the covers with his other hand. Jasper made a soft noise of surprised protest that he ignored. The sight of Jasper with flushed cheeks, his eyes wide and his mouth stretched around Vincent's cock, had a fresh heat pooling low in his belly, and he couldn't stop the moan that tore out of his chest.

Scarlet burst across Jasper's nose, which only added to the pooling heat.

"Look good like that, pet," he said, his voice rough with restraint. He slid his hand back into Jasper's hair and curled tight as he settled his other hand against Jasper's cheek and pressed his thumb in beside his cock. Then, because Jasper had enjoyed it so much, he slipped into his British accent as he said, "My perfect little slut."

Jasper let out a helpless moan, his eyes darkening almost to black as he swallowed and took Vincent in deeper.

"That's it," he murmured. "Take it all."

Jasper's fingers twitched where he'd slipped them under Vincent's hips for leverage before he dug them into Vincent's ass and lowered his head until his nose pressed into Vincent's pelvis. He immediately gagged and backed off, but Vincent kept him from pulling away completely, and the resulting whimper that vibrated around him pushed him closer to the edge than he liked.

"Already getting close. Going to swallow, pet?"

He pulled his thumb out and left a wet streak across Jasper's cheek, relenting enough to let him pull off half an inch to answer with a breathless "Yes, Sir."

"Good boy," he growled, curling his hand around the side of Jasper's throat in a brief caress before settling on the back of his neck. Hardly any pressure was needed for Jasper to put his mouth back on him. Or to take Vincent as deep as he could and hold there for a long moment.

Vincent groaned his pleasure, loud enough that Jasper's ears reddened as he pulled up to the tip and swallowed. His muscles flexed as he held off his impending orgasm, but he knew that wouldn't help for long. Another two slick glides into Jasper's mouth and a few more swirls of his tongue, and Vincent was coming. Pleasure whited his vision, his fingers twisting in Jasper's hair as he shot down his pet's throat.

For a moment everything faded beneath the intense afterglow zinging through him, and then Jasper was hovering over his chest. Eyes bright, cheeks flushed, lips slick and swollen. Vincent hummed and dragged him in for a kiss. Tasting himself on Jasper's tongue was a novelty that drew a growl out of his chest, and he rolled them over to pin Jasper down, shove a hand into his boxers, and devour his lips as he jerked him off with a few quick strokes.

Jasper arched beneath him with a desperate, pleading whine, his hips bucking into Vincent's hand before he shuddered with his own release.

Vincent didn't stop kissing him, but the intensity faded into a lazy exploration. Most of his weight settled on top of Jasper to keep him in place. Not that he ever tried to get away. Eventually Vincent moved from Jasper's lips to his neck and throat, finding the marks he'd left there to renew them.

Jasper's sighs and moans were almost enough for Vincent to get it up again, but it wasn't happening.

"Thank you, pet," he murmured between kisses.

Jasper's fingers twitched in Vincent's hair, apparently beyond a coherent response, because all he managed was a drowsy hum.

As unwilling as he was to move, Vincent finally pulled away long enough to get them cleaned up. It felt like a waste to spend their vacation sleeping when they only had a few days left, but it wasn't like he ever got enough to begin with, so he gave up on doing anything before noon and followed Jasper into sleep again.

CHAPTER 24

THE REST of their stay passed in a haze of warm pleasure.

Jasper was sore in ways he never thought possible and more relaxed and satiated than he'd ever been in his life. There'd been no further interruptions. No emergency calls. No dire texts or bad news. At least none that Vincent shared with him. He didn't want to know one way or another until they got back home. That probably made him a bigger dick than his father, but he was past the point of caring.

He threw himself completely into enjoying his vacation and having Vincent all to himself. And the sex. The sex was amazing, but that was a given.

Vincent spent an entire afternoon testing out various toys and sensations while Jasper was sprawled on the bed blindfolded. They both learned his tolerance for pain was only slightly higher than he'd previously thought and only extended to crops, clamps, or teeth. The temperature play was interesting, and the wax had been an experience all on its own, but cleaning up after was a bitch.

"Next time," Vincent had promised, "I'll shave you properly."

Jasper had mixed feelings about that, but he was willing to try almost anything once, so long as it was Vincent.

Zach and Ash invaded their cabin on their last night. Not that Jasper minded, since it was their last chance to hang out. Maybe it was because they were subs, or at least in the kink community, but it was nice being able to shimmy his way onto Vincent's lap after dinner without anyone looking at him funny.

Zach sprawled on the floor in front of the couch, rubbing his stomach with a heartfelt groan. "I ate too much."

"No one forced you to eat three helpings," Vincent said dryly, one arm resting across Jasper's thigh.

Zach lifted a hand to flip him off before dropping it back to his stomach with another exaggerated groan. "Fuuuuck."

"I can get a needle and pop you like a balloon," Jasper offered, grinning when Zach lifted his head with a gasp.

"No. You are not allowed to have the same sense of humor as him."

"Too late," Jasper retorted.

Vincent snorted. "You're just jealous because yours sucks."

"Okay, that's it," Zach said. "How dare you. I even gave you a discount on this cabin."

"Which I ignored. Be sure to clean it well. I hid the other part of the fee somewhere."

Zach muttered curses under his breath. "You try to do something nice for someone…."

"It's probably under the mattress," Ash offered from where he was tucked into the opposite side of the couch with a cup of hot tea.

Zach scoffed. "That's the last place anyone smart would hide money."

Jasper tilted his head to glance at Vincent from the corner of his eye and grinned when Vincent caught him and pinched his side.

"I didn't put it under the mattress," Vincent said, exasperated.

"Bet you're gonna move it from there as soon as we leave." Zach lifted a hand to point at Jasper. "Watch him and let me know."

Jasper raised an eyebrow. "Why would I snitch on Master Vincent?" he asked, unprepared but pleasantly surprised by the way Vincent's fingers tightened on his hip. He made the mistake of looking at him. A mistake because Vincent's eyes had darkened to molten honey, and he was watching Jasper the same way as when he tied him down to torment him.

Zach's chuckle sounded far more distant than it should have, but his words dragged Jasper back to reality. "Now you've done it. Don't go makin' out unless you plan on giving us a show."

An entirely different heat flooded Jasper. "What do you mean show?" he asked, as if an answer he wouldn't immediately perish at the mere suggestion of existed.

Zach turned his head to raise an eyebrow at him. "Oh?" he said with a soft, drawn-out and considering hum. "Whatever's good. We're not picky."

He couldn't be serious.

"Would you rather watch?"

A dying whale sound escaped Jasper's throat as he swiveled his head to stare at Ash, his body somehow getting hotter without incinerating. "What?" he wheezed.

Ash stared back with a calm expression, like they were talking about the weather. "Would you like to watch?"

The fact Vincent wasn't stopping this was as surreal as it was brain breaking. Did people really do this outside of clubs? "Watch what exactly?" he asked faintly.

"We can start with kissing and go from there."

Jasper continued staring at Ash for a long moment, then at Zach, waiting for one of them to admit they were pranking him. But they both watched him as if expecting an answer. He finally turned to Vincent and narrowed his eyes at the amused expression he found. That was enough to break through the shock. "Yes?"

Vincent's eyes softened. "Zach?" he asked without looking away from Jasper.

From the corner of his eye he saw Zach wave a hand at them. "Oh, sure. You know I'm always down for some exhibitionism. You sure your boy's not gonna have an aneurysm from watching a live porno?"

"Excuse you," Jasper scoffed, but his brain still wasn't working well enough to come up with a witty response.

Ash snorted softly as he took another sip of his tea and set the cup aside. Then he rolled to his feet with a smooth seductive ease that had Jasper's thoughts screeching off the rails and over a bridge. He walked the short distance to Zach, stood over his hips, and sank down to straddle him, his body curving forward as he leaned down for a kiss.

Jasper could only stare as they moved in a way that didn't block his view, as if they'd done this for others enough times that it was habit. The way Zach's far hand fisted Ash's hair, his other gripping Ash's hips. Ash's forearms braced on the floor beside Zach's shoulders.

He was entirely transfixed by the two of them on the floor in front of him. By the slow rock of their bodies, the soft sighs and wet kisses. It was provocative and erotic, and Jasper couldn't help but feel like he should look away, but he couldn't. Heat sparked in his gut, and he realized he'd completely lost his sense of Vincent when a hand settled against the inside of his thigh.

He didn't resist as Vincent adjusted him so he was sitting with his back to Vincent's chest, his legs resting on either side of him. He became all too aware of Vincent then. The solid line of a firm body pressed all along his back, the sharp, pleasant scent of his cologne, the possessive grip of Vincent's hands as they settled on Jasper's hips and inched towards his groin.

Jasper let his head fall back against Vincent's shoulder without taking his eyes off the show. "You're really okay with this?" he asked softly.

Vincent hummed and dragged his nose up the side of Jasper's neck. "I am if you are."

Jasper wasn't sure of anything. That was the problem. But this wasn't much different from what he'd seen in the club, even if it was way more intimate, and he couldn't possibly pretend he wasn't staring. Which seemed to be the point. He was still a little worried that Vincent would see them making out and realize he really wanted more or different subs, but the warm hand sliding under his shirt to rest against his stomach mostly extinguished that fear.

Vincent's soft words in his ear obliterated the rest. "They look good," Vincent whispered, "but they're not nearly as bratty or vocal as you. You're mine."

Jasper whimpered, closing his eyes as Vincent's teeth dragged against his earlobe before trailing a line down his neck.

"Do you want to watch them do more than kiss?"

His eyes flew open, though whether it was fear of missing out or panic of actually seeing it, he wasn't sure. Probably both. He'd never felt so far in over his head as he did right then, but maybe that was okay. He took a deep breath and tried to calm his thudding heartbeat. That was only embarrassment. Mostly. Made worse since he was sure he was the only one having a minor freak-out about this.

He couldn't deny it was as hot as it was strange, and he certainly couldn't hide his body's reaction, but the bulge forming against his lower back was reassuring. He wet his lips with the tip of his tongue, admiring the lithe lines of Zach and Ash moving against each other. "What are you okay with?" he asked, tilting his head enough to rest his temple against Vincent's cheek. He almost expected Vincent to say he was good with whatever Jasper wanted, as usual, but he'd been more willing to share what he wanted since they got here.

"So long as they stay over there, I'm fine with letting them get off." Vincent flexed his fingers on Jasper's thigh. "Maybe stick with hand jobs rather than watching them have sex."

"Yeah," Jasper breathed. That sounded good. Not that he'd ever admit it, but Zach was right; he wasn't sure he could handle watching them get fully naked and have sex right there in front of him.

"No boning. Got it," Zach murmured, flashing them a brief grin before lifting his hand and bringing it down against Ash's ass with a resounding slap. Ash arched with a moan, grinding his hips harder against Zach.

Jasper was distracted enough watching Zach get a hand in Ash's pants that he didn't notice Vincent doing the same to him until Vincent's palm was pressed against his aching cock. He let out a strangled sound somewhere between a yelp and a moan and latched on to Vincent's forearm. "Not fair, Sir," he said, though he couldn't quite decide which part.

Vincent must have seen through him because his only response was a soft huff of hot breath against Jasper's neck. His other hand inched up Jasper's chest until he reached a nipple, and then Jasper was helpless to do anything but hold on and watch, pleasure and the fluttery excitement of trying something new blanking everything else.

His breaths got shorter as Ash moved faster, bucking into Zach's hand, his head tipped back, mouth open on near-silent gasps. Zach was murmuring something, but his voice was low enough Jasper couldn't make out the words over the rushing in his ears. It must have been something dirty, because Ash's flush of pleasure darkened, and then he let out a soft, sharp groan and went still, his lips twitching with his obvious orgasm.

Vincent's fingers twitched against Jasper, then wrapped around him as he began stroking. Jasper bit his lip hard to stifle his moan.

Zach pulled his hand out of Ash's pants and lifted it to his lips, eyes half-lidded as he slowly dragged his tongue over his fingers one by one. Ash muttered something that sounded taunting, and Zach laughed, sprawling with his hands above his head as Ash worked his pants open to return the favor. Once Ash got a hand inside he shoved Zach's shirt up and leaned down to sink his teeth into a nipple.

Jasper winced in sympathy as Zach let out a pained hiss, pleasure zinging through Jasper when Vincent followed suit and pinched his nipple. Vincent's lips lightly brushing his ear sent shivers down his spine, and he pushed his hips into the teasing pressure with a pleading whine. The answering chuckle wasn't reassuring in the least. He knew he should be worried about what Vincent might have planned, but he knew he'd most likely enjoy it regardless, and Vincent surely knew that too, the dick.

On the floor Zach arched with a loud moan, his wrists pinned together by one of Ash's hands while the other pumped quickly out of immediate view. A few moments later Zach let out a gasping shout as he came, then grunted as Ash slumped on top of him and tipped to the side in a boneless heap.

Jasper barely had time to start to feel weird about the entire situation before Vincent's hand moved in earnest, stroking him without pulling him out of his pants completely. His other hand continued tormenting Jasper's nipples, and as much as he enjoyed it, he doubted he'd be able to get off with an audience. Especially when they both glanced over with interest.

But the moment Vincent slid his hand from under Jasper's shirt and wrapped it around his throat with a growled, "Come," Jasper was gone, a bright burst of pleasure shoving him over the edge.

He slumped in Vincent's lap with a drawn-out groan, a small distant part of him embarrassed beyond belief that he came in front of others, but he felt too good to care. After a few moments, he finally found his senses enough to nuzzle against Vincent's neck. "What about you?"

"I can wait until we're alone."

Zach chuckled. "How rude. Kicking us out after we put on such a good show for you."

"I didn't tell you to leave."

He waved a hand and yawned. "Uh-huh. We can take a hint. I'm about to slip into a food-and-sex coma anyway."

"Take the leftovers with you."

"Oooh, yes, please." Zach yawned again and groaned as he picked himself up, then offered a hand to Ash to pull him to his feet. He tossed a wink at Jasper on his way to the kitchen.

Ash fixed his pants with his back to them before turning to face them. "Was good seeing you again," he said. "And meeting you," he added to Jasper. He stepped away, stopped, and turned back, quickly leaning in to kiss them each on the cheek. "Visit again soon." Then he headed for the door.

Jasper touched his cheek in surprise, glancing at Vincent, who looked as shocked as he felt.

"Seems he's taken a liking to you," Vincent said dryly, which was weird since Jasper had spent more time with Zach than Ash.

Zach returned with the leftovers and a few bags of what food they hadn't used up. "Text when you get home."

"Sure."

"And don't be a ghost from now on," he said, pointing an accusatory finger at Vincent. Then he wiggled the rest of them at Jasper. "You have my number if you wanna chat." Then he was gone, the door clicking shut loud in the ensuing silence.

Jasper was suddenly all too aware of his current state, and Vincent's, which was still pressed against his lower back. "Whelp," he said. "That was fun. Time for bed." He wiggled off Vincent's lap and made it all the way to the top of the stairs before Vincent caught him with a low growl. He yelped as his feet left the ground, but he was laughing when he hit the bed.

"You really think I'm done with you?" Vincent asked mildly, manhandling Jasper with an ease that made his stomach swoop like he was on the zip line all over again. He only clued in to Vincent's plans when his shoulders were lined up with the edge of the bed, his head hovering over the edge. He swallowed hard and stared up at Vincent who was standing with a hand resting on Jasper's throat. He didn't wait for an order before reaching for the button and zipper of Vincent's jeans. Getting them open while essentially upside down took some finagling, but he managed.

"Hands behind your back, pet."

He swallowed again to stifle a whimper and shifted back and forth on the bed to get his hands under him.

Vincent caressed Jasper's cheek with a thumb before sliding it across his lips, and then the hot, blunt tip of his cock followed, pressing into Jasper's mouth.

Jasper closed his eyes with a moan, lifting a knee for balance even though he couldn't possibly go anywhere. Vincent's hand didn't leave his throat. It wasn't anything more than a warm, barely there weight, but it was still enough to spark a fresh wave of heat in him. The way Vincent relentlessly took his own pleasure, sliding into Jasper's throat, triggering his gag reflex over and over again until tears stung his eyes, had him hard and aching again by the time Vincent pulled away.

He was still trying to catch his breath when he realized Vincent hadn't come, and a soft needy whine escaped him as Vincent dragged him across the bed far enough for his legs to hang off the edge instead.

Vincent made quick work of Jasper's pants and boxers, lubed himself up, lifted Jasper's legs over his shoulders, and braced a knee on the bed as he slowly pushed inside. He leaned down to press wet kisses across Jasper's chest, leaving marks in his wake. "You've been so good, pet," he murmured, glancing up to meet Jasper's eyes as he lazily circled his tongue around a nipple. "Not only today. The entire time we've been here you've been amazing."

Heat that had nothing to do with the dick inside him pulsed through Jasper and left him breathless.

"More than amazing," Vincent murmured. "More than I could have asked for. You've been perfect."

Jasper keened, pulled his hands from underneath him, buried them in Vincent's hair, and yanked him in for a messy kiss.

Vincent returned it as readily as he ever did without missing a single thrust. Even when he tugged one of Jasper's hands free to pin above his head, he kept up the steady pace.

"You're perfect," Jasper gasped. "So good to me, Sir. Master Vincent." Vincent made a choked-off, growling sound and slammed into Jasper, which was what he'd hoped for. He tightened his grip on Vincent's hair with a gasped, "Yes!" and proceeded to urge Vincent into fucking him into oblivion.

When they were finally spent and properly settled in bed countless minutes later, he tucked himself against Vincent's chest with a deep sigh of contentment. Rather than passing out like he usually did, he found himself listening to Vincent's breathing as it evened out and slowed.

He hated that they'd be up in a few hours to go back home to face reality. He'd be more than happy to move into the cabin indefinitely, getting to know Zach and Ash while he broadened his kink horizons with Vincent. If only Vincent didn't have a club to run and Jasper didn't have his final year of college coming. Maybe they could take another vacation once he graduated, before he got sucked into the EMT courses.

He tipped his head back with a sigh, studying Vincent's face in the dim light. Once he was sure Vincent was really asleep, he whispered the words he couldn't dare say while Vincent was awake to hear them.

"I think I'm falling in love with you."

CHAPTER 25

THEIR FLIGHT back home was uneventful, especially since Vincent had kept his grandfather's jet to use rather than deal with a commercial airline again. They spent the flight alternating between kissing and dozing, enjoying what little time they had left before returning to their real-life obligations.

They made it all the way to the car Vincent's driver had waiting for them and were exiting the airport traffic when his phone chimed with a text from Amber.

He's gone the funeral is next week.

Vincent stared at it long enough for Jasper to notice.

"What's wrong?"

Vincent hit the button to shut off the screen and blew out a slow breath before turning to Jasper. "Are we considered back home now?"

Jasper's face did a complicated twist of emotions before he let out a resigned sigh. "I guess. Why?"

He pulled the message back up. "Amber texted an update," he said and held the phone out.

Jasper didn't take it immediately, eyeing it like it might bite his hand off. He waited until the screen dimmed before holding his hand out, and he stared at the screen without reacting for several long moments. When he finally moved, it was to unbuckle and shift across the seat to lean heavily against Vincent. "I don't want to go," he whispered.

"You don't have to." Vincent still made a mental note to make sure he had no plans that day in case Jasper changed his mind. The phone chimed with another text and Jasper stiffened against his side.

Vincent tugged the phone free and narrowed his eyes.

We need to talk we're waiting outside.

"I'll tell them to leave," Vincent said tightly, pressing the Call button. He didn't appreciate being ambushed, certainly not when he'd been planning on enjoying his own shower and bed and a last lazy afternoon with Jasper.

"Don't," Jasper murmured as the call connected.

He hit Mute rather than answer Amber's defensive greeting. "We can get a hotel room for the night," he offered.

Jasper tipped his head back with a tired smile. "Let's just get this over with."

He unmuted the phone long enough to say "We'll be there in twenty," then disconnected without waiting for a response.

Sure enough, Amber's car was sitting at the curb when they pulled up. Vincent didn't know how long they'd been waiting, and he didn't care. He hadn't shared their new flight time with anyone except Jasper, and the petty part of him wished he'd pushed their arrival time back to late afternoon.

They grabbed their bags and headed inside. A pile of mail waited on the hall table, courtesy of the cleaning service that would have come by the day before. A small rectangular package caught his eye, and he regretted that now certainly wasn't the time to open it. He set his bags to the side to deal with later and turned to the door; Amber and Noah had followed them in.

He shut the door, intending to leave them and Jasper to discuss whatever family business they thought was so important, but Jasper's hand in his stopped him from going anywhere. He glanced over, raising an eyebrow in question. Jasper merely tightened his hold and pulled him to the dining room. He sat when Jasper still didn't let go, ignoring Amber's clearly disgruntled expression and fighting a smug one of his own when Jasper pointedly lifted their hands to rest on the table.

"I'm not going to the funeral if that's why you're here."

Amber flinched and turned her attention to Jasper. "Jas—"

"Just tell him," Noah interrupted, sounding bored. "I've got better things to do."

Amber shot him a look like she wanted to call him on that, but she relented. She set her purse in her lap and pulled out some papers, and Vincent suddenly had an even worse feeling about this. "I got the DNA test results."

Jasper leaned back in his chair. Vincent couldn't blame him; he wasn't sure if he'd want to know the truth in this kind of situation either.

"I tested all of us."

"You what?" Jasper snapped, surging to his feet, his blunt nails biting into Vincent's hand. "I told you I didn't want to be involved."

She tossed the papers to the middle of the table. "I needed yours for confirmation," she replied, unapologetic. "We're all half siblings."

Vincent squeezed Jasper's hand when he felt the tremble that ran through him. Jasper didn't say anything, his other hand braced on the table while anger warred with half a dozen other emotions on his face. "Just so I understand," Vincent said quietly. "You did a DNA test on Jasper without his consent?"

Amber straightened with a wary glance his way.

"I told her not to," Noah said. "I'd offer my statement as a witness if you want to sue her, or whatever, but I doubt my word would be worth anything. Congrats, bro," he added, pushing to his feet. "You two share your father, and I share her inheritance. If you wanna get drunk about it, hit me up. Let's go before they call the cops on you." He turned and headed for the door.

Amber was slow to follow, but she finally got to her feet, lingering beside the table like she wanted to say something. A quick glance at each of them and she decided against it. She left the papers and followed Noah out.

Vincent kept silent for several moments after the door closed, waiting for Jasper to do or say anything, but he was still standing there, eyes fixed on the papers. Finally, he slumped forward with a shaky breath.

"I can't go back home," he murmured, an empty quality to his voice that Vincent didn't like in the least.

"No," he agreed. "You shouldn't have to." Amber of all people was one of the last he'd expect to violate someone's trust like that. He had to wonder if she broke trust so easily within scenes, but unless she started playing with club members rather than her fiancé, it wasn't his business. "You can stay here as long as you need."

This certainly wasn't how he imagined offering to let Jasper move in would go, but it couldn't be helped. He squeezed Jasper's fingers and stood, then guided him upstairs, unsurprised when he readily crawled into bed and burrowed under the covers.

Vincent waited until he'd fallen asleep before getting up and adjusting the thermostat back to his preferred 71 degrees. He grabbed his suitcase and took it to the washing machine to get started on laundry, then sorted the mail. Mostly spam, a few bills, Jasper's collar. The pictures likely weren't even ready to mail yet, since he'd ordered specific sizes, but he was still disappointed not to see them.

He took the collar up to tuck into a drawer of his dresser, then joined Jasper on the bed with his phone. He'd need to get a key made, but they could do that tomorrow. For now he put an order in for sushi to be delivered for dinner and spent the rest of the afternoon catching up on work.

CHAPTER 26

JASPER'S RESOLVE not to go to the funeral held out clear until the morning of, when the guilt finally won. It'd been as horrible as he'd imagined it would be, and he left before the service concluded, grateful beyond belief that Vincent was there since he wouldn't have been able to get away fast enough if he'd had to rely on Amber.

She hadn't mentioned anything about the fact he hadn't been home the past week, and the guilt about imposing on Vincent was getting worse every day. It didn't come close to overriding the anger and loathing he now felt for Amber, though. He wasn't sure he could ever trust her enough to live there again, but he couldn't barge into Vincent's life.

Their vacation had been amazing, but even he knew that wasn't a reasonable excuse to move in together. Not like he had many options. He certainly couldn't afford an apartment, even if he wanted one, not with his last year about to start. If he was lucky he could save up enough to get his license and pay for his exams by next year, have a steady job by the one after that, but getting a car and his own place to live were completely beyond him at the moment.

Maybe Vincent would cosign a lease for him? That sounded like the best plan, if he could only afford the rent. No point in Vincent helping if he'd end up paying for two homes.

He was saved from his existential crisis by Vincent calling for him from downstairs. He rolled off the bed where he was most definitely wallowing and found Vincent at the dining table with some packages. "Yeah?"

Vincent stood behind a chair and motioned for Jasper to sit in it. "I have some things for you."

"Oh?" He sat and stared at the large thick envelope and smaller rectangular box.

"The pictures Ash took came in."

And just like that, Jasper knew his face was crimson. "I don't need to see them."

Vincent snorted and mussed Jasper's hair with one hand as he picked up the envelope with the other. "I'd like to put at least one of these in the main room of the club. You can pick which one. Or I'll keep them to my office if you prefer."

"You can't be serious," he whispered. Even if Vincent had said before that's what he wanted, Jasper hadn't quite believed he'd go through with it. He watched as Vincent opened the envelope and pulled out a stack of professionally developed pictures. "Oh," he breathed, startled by the one on top. It was him and Vincent, staring at each other, obviously about to or just finished kissing. The soft light made Vincent's eyes even more golden.

The colors had obviously been edited. He didn't remember the trees being so green, or the streaks of early morning sunlight being so clearly defined through the leaves, but it was beautiful.

"That one's going in my office," Vincent said.

Jasper tilted his head to eye Vincent. He had a feeling if he didn't mark any of them as an Absolutely Do Not Put This Up, they'd all end up on the wall somewhere. Vincent left him to decide as he started on lunch. Jasper watched long enough to know he was making sandwiches before turning back to the pictures.

The black-and-white ones were stunning, cropped in a way that cut off their faces to provide anonymity. If he hadn't known he was looking at himself, he wouldn't have thought twice about seeing them hanging in the club. The more he thought about it the more he warmed to the idea.

Vincent basically wanted to put him on display. A year ago he would have balked at the idea, but now…? If Vincent wanted to publicly claim him, he was okay with that.

"Any of these that don't show my face are fine," he said quietly, his attention lingering on the color one of him and Vincent, eyes locked on each other. He remembered the moment. It was hard to forget when he'd been tied to a tree and about to be blindfolded and posed for photos while mostly naked. He was sure it'd been a *moment*, even without trying to read too much into their expressions.

"Yeah?" Vincent asked, glancing over with an eyebrow raised in surprise.

Jasper shrugged. "Unless someone sees me standing shirtless beside them they won't be able to tell it's me, right?"

"Probably."

He nodded and carefully slid the pictures back into the envelope, then poked the other package. "Can I open this?"

Vincent hummed and turned away from the sandwiches. “Yes,” he said, wiping his hands on a towel on his way over. Jasper expected him to say something else, but he only stood beside the table and waited.

His stomach did a weird little flip-flop. He pulled the box closer and got it open, then stared at the black links for a moment as he worked out what it was. “Is this….” He picked it up, running his fingers over the smooth twists of metal. It wasn’t anything like the collars he saw every weekend at the club, but surely Vincent wouldn’t give him a necklace without some kind of meaning behind it.

Vincent shifted beside the table and cleared his throat. “It’s a day collar.”

Jasper finally looked up. “Day collar?”

“Most of the collars you see are specifically for scenes. This,” he said, reaching out to touch the collar, “is meant to be worn all the time.”

“All the time?” Heat clenched in his stomach, and he sucked in a ragged breath. “You’re really collaring me?”

Vincent stepped closer, lifting his hand from the collar to tangle in Jasper’s hair. “Yes,” he said with a low growl that didn’t ease the clenching heat in the least. A soft whine built in Jasper’s throat and escaped when Vincent tightened his fingers and tugged. “You’re mine, Jas. If having a collar around your neck all day every day as proof of that helps convince you I’m not letting you go, all the better.”

This couldn’t be real. Barely six months ago he’d been single and brokenhearted, needing something he could barely name.

“You can officially move in, if you want.”

Then he met Vincent, had an amazing night learning exactly what he’d been missing, and started down the path that lead to this moment of Vincent laying a real and tangible claim on him.

“Are you going to say something?”

“Yes,” he breathed. “Please.” He lifted the box in a wordless request for Vincent to put the collar on him.

Vincent straightened and picked up the collar. The clasp wasn’t the usual hook but one that screwed together. It was heavier than Jasper expected when it settled around his neck, the metal cool against his skin.

He hooked two fingers over the chain and felt something release inside him as the metal warmed.

Once the collar was fastened, Vincent straightened and hooked his own finger in the black and silver rings dangling over the hollow of Jasper's throat. "It looks good," he murmured, giving an experimental tug.

The bolt of hot pleasure was expected, but it still coaxed a moan out of Jasper. The thought of Vincent always having an easy way to drag him closer was as thrilling as it was worrying.

He dropped his hands to his lap and tipped his head back. "All yours, Master Vincent," he said and was rewarded with a slow kiss that left him breathless and unable to think of anything but how utterly lucky he was. What more could he possibly ask for?

Epilogue

JASPER STARTED the washer and grabbed the basket of dried clothes, using his hip to shut the dryer door. A month since he'd officially moved in. A month since he gathered up his meager belongings from both his old home and Amber's and put them away in the spare room Vincent had given him.

He didn't know what was being done with his father's house. He'd left it to Amber to sort out since she was technically his half sister, which was still difficult to wrap his head around. The only inheritance was debt, so he'd taken his personal possessions and washed his hands of the rest.

The only good thing to come out of the past few months, other than his living situation, was that he and Noah had reconnected. His brother was trying to piece his life back together, trying to get clean of the drugs even if he refused to give up alcohol. It was a start at least. He even came over to hang out every once in a while, though Jasper had made it clear if he brought drugs or alcohol into Vincent's home, they were done. It was a tentative start to getting his own life where he wanted it to be.

Classes started in a couple of weeks, and he was almost used to having access to a driver. Vincent had hired a second until Jasper got a license and car of his own, and he suspected that would happen sooner than he could afford if the not-so-subtle questions about what kind of cars Jasper liked was any indication. He'd promised to kick Vincent's ass if he bought him a new car and only got an amused twitch of lips in return.

He doubted he'd ever get used to how rich Vincent was, much less receiving expensive gifts, and he definitely didn't want to take advantage like Adam had, but *maybe* letting Vincent buy him things once in a while was okay. Might have even been nice when he wasn't having a panic attack over price tags.

He hooked a finger over his collar as he turned, the metal warm from his body heat. Every time he thought he was getting used to it, Vincent would hook a leash to it, or his finger, or attach a charm or something to the circle, and the weight would be noticeable all over again.

The door to Vincent's office opened behind him and he turned back, stepped in close, and leaned in to steal a kiss.

Vincent hummed softly and slipped an arm around Jasper's waist, trailing a kiss down Jasper's neck and lingering near the collar.

Jasper tipped his head to the side to give Vincent better access, his eyes snagging on the door at the end of the hall. The door that was always locked the few times he'd gotten nosy enough to explore. "Sir," he said.

"Hmm?"

"What's in there?" he asked, waiting for Vincent to lift his head to motion to the door with his chin. The way Vincent stilled caught his attention. For a fleeting moment he wondered if it was some kind of murder room, and now that he'd finally found out Vincent's deep dark secret, he was next.

Vincent sighed and stepped back. "You may as well see," he said, sounding resigned. He stepped into his office and retrieved a key from the drawer of his desk, then headed down the hall to unlock the door. Then he stood there, his hand gripping the knob without turning it.

Jasper's eyebrows inched up when nearly a full minute passed without his opening the door. Was it somehow *worse* than a murder room? "Sir?" he asked softly. "You don't have to show me…."

"No." Vincent heaved a deep sigh like he was going to his execution, which made absolutely no sense, and finally opened the door. He stopped, waiting beside it like he planned to escape the moment Jasper stepped into the definitely-probably-not-a-murder room.

Jasper hesitated, but his curiosity won within a few seconds, and he moved forward. "What the—" The laundry basket slipped free of his fingers, but that was a distant concern. Not nearly as important as the room he'd stepped into.

Lining the walls and scattered through the center were racks of clothes. A hoarder amount of clothes. Except they were all arranged neatly. Not just neatly, he realized as the shock gave way to amazed interest. They were clearly arranged by some kind of system, but it wasn't until he found an actual authentic-looking cowboy outfit, complete with spurs, hat, and lasso hanging next to a similar one with an old-fashioned star badge that had Sheriff stamped into the metal that he finally realized what this was.

"Holy shit," he breathed. "You weren't kidding when you said you liked role-play."

It was like standing in the middle of a Goodwill. Rather, it was more like a rich person's version of a Spirit Halloween.

He made a slow circuit of the room, finding everything from see-through harem outfits to fantasy-style tunics to an honest-to-God Batman costume. Uniforms from plumber to policeman to fireman with an oxygen tank. When he turned back towards the door, he saw the wall to the side of it was filled with shelves full of accessories. Crowns and rings, belts and sashes, and several different pairs of shoes and boots that could work with dozens of outfits. Then there was Vincent, still standing beside the door like he expected Jasper to run screaming at any moment.

"There's a small fortune in this room, isn't there?" he asked.

A pained look crossed Vincent's face. "Yes."

Jasper nodded as he reached Vincent and lightly gripped the bottom of his shirt. "Well, this makes it easier," he said, grinning when Vincent eyed him in confusion. "Ever since I got a taste of being a prince, I've had *ideas*. Like, instead of being married off to a princess, maybe her debatably evil father decides to marry me instead."

Vincent huffed a laugh and settled his hands on Jasper's hips, where they quickly slid down to grope his ass. "It doesn't bother you?"

Jasper tilted his head, glancing around the room again before shrugging. "Not really. Kinda weird. Kinda hot. Can I see you in the Batman outfit?"

Vincent laughed and backed him into the room.

"But if you try to put me in a Robin outfit, I'm out."

"Don't worry. There's a cat burglar one that's all sleek leather."

"Oooh, *mreow*."

Keep Reading for an Excerpt from *Wild's Scar*
Book #2 in the Elemental Thrones Series
by Saria Bryant

CHAPTER 1

FUCKING FATE bonds.

He was too old to deal with one appearing on him.

Vesryn was over six hundred years old, and he'd served the royal family for more than five of those centuries. He'd taken countless lovers through the years and had even bedded Prince Callith—now King Callith—on numerous occasions, but he'd never found someone he wanted to share the rest of his life with.

Vesryn was content with his role in the kingdom, and he was thankful his only duty was to protect Synne. If he had the weight of the kingdom on his shoulders, they'd likely all be dead from a civil war.

He couldn't help flexing his fingers, staring at the shimmering red thread that stretched up to a higher floor. He couldn't feel it, but his finger insisted there was a hint of a tingling sensation, as if it were on the verge of falling asleep.

"Vesryn?"

He glanced at Synne, returning her raised eyebrow with one of his own. "Yes, Princess?" He restrained a smile when she wrinkled her nose at him.

"Are you ill?"

He couldn't quite fight back his scowl. "No," he said, but her brow twitched higher in a familiar expression of disbelief.

"You should get some rest."

Vesryn started to say he was fine, but the threat of a pang beneath his ribs stayed his tongue. He was well accustomed to the discomfort that came with lying, but it was still never pleasant. The worse the lie, the deeper and sharper the ache. Truth be told, he did need rest. He hadn't been sleeping well, kept awake at night by the thread on his finger. Since Synne could be far more stubborn than her older brother when she chose, he swept a low bow and stepped back.

"As you wish." He turned and motioned for two other guards to move in and take his place. Then he headed out of the throne room and stopped by Duaia's office, surprised to find her at her desk for once.

He rapped his knuckles against the door to get her attention before stepping inside. “Can you assign someone to Synne for a few days?”

Duaia eyed him in surprise, sitting back and tucking stray wisps of bright red hair behind her ear. “Shouldn’t be a problem. Elwin has been asking for something other than prison duty.”

Elwin was a good choice. He was levelheaded and had the quick reflexes innate to all feline beastkin, and he was part of Callith’s kingsguard. With the king currently out of the city, the kingsguard were spread out to help with the patrols and city guard.

Vesryn nodded his thanks and stepped back, escaping before she could try to pry and stubbornly ignoring the twinge of guilt. He might be centuries older than Duaia, but as the only sorceress on this side of the Wound, he knew better than to catch her attention. She could be as ruthless as Synne when it came to protecting her own, even if it meant berating someone until they wept.

With the sudden lack of immediate responsibility, exhaustion pressed in on him. He intended to go to his room, shower, and try to sleep. Instead, he found himself following the Fate string and stopped outside the closed door of the fae’s room.

This was a terrible idea. What could Fate possibly want with Vesryn, an elf with a fractured magical core? He had no talent for the sun magic most elves were gifted with. The only magic he had ever been able to control was fire, but he couldn’t even start a fire with condensed sunlight. No, the fire had to already exist; then he could call on the flames and manipulate them. And only natural flames answered to him. He’d been of no help at all when the Black Sun set fires to their granary and the library and the temple, the alchemical-borne flames tearing through everything far quicker than a natural fire.

He may have been one of the most skilled with a blade, but he paled against the warriors who’d been lost in the war. Surely there were others who could offer more.

He lowered his hand and turned away.

If he was to speak to the fae for the first time, he’d need honey.

CHAPTER 2

FLESH WAS a prison.

The sense of time he'd lost during the three centuries when his essence was trapped in the ley lines returned to suffocate him now.

Every moment was filled with the swirl of air in his lungs, the pulse of blood in his veins, the rough clothes chafing his skin, the sharp bite of itches in his wings. Even the blissful taste of honey bordered on too sweet, the thick substance lingering on the back of his tongue long after he'd eaten it.

The only relief was the slow, steady pulse of the ylren tree around him. It was old, far older than him, the deep, lingering pool of fae magic in its roots a balm against his senses. The sweetness of its blossoms was as nostalgic as it was a painful reminder of everything lost because of him. Because of one moment of weakness.

He didn't have the excuse of youthful folly either. He'd known the risks, knew humans were rarely trustworthy, even before they stole the throne. Even when they'd had only the ability to work basic magics, they were disturbingly greedy for more.

Not that fae were better, but at least with fae, it was expected that the glint of silver was a dagger and not a coin or trinket. Fae were masters at twisting words and meanings, but the human ability to lie was as fascinating as it was dangerous, especially when they could lie even to themselves.

As much as he might want to stay here, he didn't belong. Elves may be descended from the first fae to tame this realm, but they weren't his people. He had no people in this realm, and after what he'd wrought here, he may well be executed if he tried to cross into the fae realm.

Except he had to restore the balance first.

Already the ley lines were in flux without him restraining the wild magic. With the last piece of the throne completely destroyed, the thin connection holding the balance of elements in check, the connection that Draekor had manipulated and violated, was broken. Wild magic would overcome the other elements, return them to chaos, and tear this realm apart, reducing it to the land ravaged by violent storms and noxious air it had been before his ancestors tamed it. Before the Second Daughter of the Queen of the Wild Court stepped through the veil and separated the threads of magic into their elements, grounding them in their respective Thrones—Light, Frost, Sea, Nature, Air, and Wild.

Humans called it Shadow when they stole his family's throne, but his people called it Wild. The shadows might have been part of that, but he'd ensured the humans never learned to tap into the creation magics, or the ability to reshape the realm. To call on the earth to form mountains or valleys, or for the skies to flood the land, or the deep, hot pools of liquid rock to burst free of the confines of the earth, or to ask the seasons to change before their time.

Shadows were the weakest essence of wild magic. A cloak or a shroud, or the ability to step across a great distance. Even still, the humans had turned them into a formidable weapon, and they would have discovered their ability to harness all the Wilds if he hadn't stopped them. But even that came with a price, and he saw the consequences of his choice every time he looked past the city walls and into the Wound—the barren, magic-void, lifeless wasteland that had ripped across the center of the continent when Sorren sacrificed him.

If there was to be any hope of healing the land, the Wild Throne had to be restored and placed on the largest ley line of the realm, but he had no idea how to do that. There had only ever been one Wild Throne created, long before his birth, and the humans had tainted it, filled it with shadows, before the Sun King destroyed the last piece of it.

He brushed his fingers against the delicate petals of a ylren blossom before turning and sitting on the window seat. This was his mistake, his responsibility. He was fae, a descendant of Lilithani, Queen of the Wild Court. He was—

He was….

What was his name?

He could remember everything that Draekor had done to him, everything Draekor's ancestors had forced him to do, but everything before he gave his name to a human was a blur, and even his name wouldn't reveal itself.

Truth be told, that was a relief. He couldn't be trusted with it. If he didn't know his own name, he couldn't make the same mistake again, and Fate, whoever the Fate was now, seemed intent he do exactly that.

He glanced at the Fate bond wrapped around his little finger, absently rubbing his thumb against the faint shimmer of magic and wondering if it would vanish if he cut off his finger. If it would linger there, as if attached to a phantom limb, or if it would simply attach to the next finger.

Fate usually didn't meddle in the affairs of fae, but he supposed he deserved this. Maybe it was punishment. If not for being naive enough to give his name to a human and allowing himself to be enslaved by them, then perhaps for staining his hands with the blood of his family. Or maybe because he'd placed that fake Fate bond on Haru and Sorren that ensured the end of Draekor's bloodline.

He knew what Fate wanted. Or thought he knew.

With the backlash of his resurrection, the veil he'd sealed Ages ago had blown wide open. He could feel some of the tears from here, open wounds where the magic of the fae realm was already seeping back into this one. While that meant restoring life to the ylren trees, it also meant the creatures there could once again roam this one. After so long existing with their absence, this realm was not prepared for that.

The light knock at the door drew his attention from the glimmer of red around his finger. He looked up as the door opened, expecting the usual servant with food and a bit of honey. Instead, it was an elf.

A surprisingly attractive elf, and the elf he was Fate bound to.

He stilled, cursing his wings when they shifted, the faint rustle of feathers loud in the silence.

The elf set a tray of food and a jar of honey down with a bow of his head before stepping back. When the elf opened his mouth after a long moment of silence, he expected a plea for a chance to spend time together, to talk or walk or fuck. Instead, the elf said, "I'm sorry—"

"Leave." The word was out of his mouth before he understood what the elf said, but that didn't matter. He had no interest in getting to know anyone, elf or otherwise. Even if he remembered, he certainly never intended to grant his name to another soul of this realm, so the Fate bond between them could never amount to anything more than an unfulfilled promise.

The elf flinched as if struck, but he didn't protest. Merely dipped into a polite bow and backed out of the room.

He waited several long moments to ensure no one else entered before standing from his perch in the window. He surveyed the tray, recognizing most of the fresh fruits as ones originating from the fae realm. The news that some of this city's crops had changed in the days before Draekor's attempted coup wasn't surprising; he'd been losing his grasp on his own essence at that point, and his fae magic had seeped out where it could.

He picked up one of the red fruits with soft skin and bit into it, his teeth easily ripping through the flesh. He'd forgotten what eating was like, but he was sure it had never been so tedious before. After three hundred years stuck as an entity of magic while the raw power of the ley lines slowly burned and ripped his essence to pieces, he'd forgotten most everything of having a corporeal form.

He licked a trickle of sweet juice from his wrist, savoring the subtle flavors as he methodically ate through the food provided, saving the small jar of honey for last. He dipped his finger into the golden substance and licked it clean, then vanished the jar from this plane into his hollow with the others. His personal holding space was empty aside from the jars of honey and some scattered seeds from the fruits he'd eaten.

He wasn't sure how long he would stay here, but he intended to have a sizable collection of honey to sustain him when he left.

For now, he needed a name.

Aster was a whisper in the back of his mind, but that name wasn't his. Aster had died long before he took possession of the human's body, his essence swallowed by the fragment of Draekor that had survived in his descendant's bloodline.

He'd underestimated Draekor's will to survive when he'd orchestrated Sorren's death; he hadn't thought to eliminate distant relatives as well. But there'd be no more coming back now; he'd made sure to destroy the last of Draekor's essence when he took this body for his own.

He moved to the large balcony and hopped onto the railing, gripping it with his talons before crouching and staring out over the city, wings spread to keep his balance.

The stench of iron and silver from the large building across the river left an acrid burn in his nose, though the people here would likely need it for protection soon enough. The bustle of the people below was a distant chorus of voices, merchants shouting and children laughing. The scent of fresh baked bread and cut herbs and roasting meat drifted on the air.

He was intimately familiar with the heartbeat of this city, but it was different seeing it from above.

He tipped his head back, closing his eyes and letting the sun warm his face. He wanted to take to the skies, but he doubted his wings or magic were strong enough yet to carry him. If he tried now, he'd surely plummet to the ground, and while it might not kill him, it would be painful.

He opened his eyes, staring at the clouds and breathing in the hint of rain. The promise of life.

He might be fae, one with the curse of the raven wings, but he doubted he would live an immortal life.

That would be a suitable name.

Fey. Fated to die.

Saria has been an avid reader since childhood and a fan fiction writer since middle school. They enjoy traveling and exploring and learning about other cultures and languages.

They are constantly dreaming up new ways to torment their characters and feeding a caffeine addiction.

Their favorite stories are M/M/+ relationships with a healthy dose of angst and drama with an HEA. When not reading or writing, they can usually be found watching anime or playing video games.

Saria can be found on Twitter/Instagram/Tumblr/Bluesky @sariabryant.

If You
LET ME

TOUCH OF LEATHER •BOOK 1•

SARIA BRYANT

Touch of Leather: Book One

When Jasper is invited by his cousin to a kink club, he's all too eager for a chance to try something new, especially when Vincent, a gorgeous man in a suit, offers to bring his fantasy to life. After an amazing scene together and his first true taste of kink, Jasper is hooked. What starts as a one-night-a-week exploration quickly turns into a request for more and a contract between them.

Having given up on finding a sub for himself after his last disaster of a relationship, Vincent is surprised to find himself drawn to Jasper. More than the contradiction of shy young man and bratty personality, Jasper seems made specifically to submit to Vincent. Their chemistry is amazing, and Vincent is willing to try again. The only problem is Jasper's self-doubt and near-desperate need to please.

Scan the QR code below to order

SHADOW'S
WOUND
ELEMENTAL THRONES
BOOK 1
SARIA BRYANT

Elemental Thrones: Book One

With the realm teetering on the brink of magical annihilation, Callith Ratearynn, the reluctant heir to the Sun Throne, is thrust into power centuries too soon. With his father dead and corruption tearing the kingdom apart at the seams, Cal must battle rising racial tensions and unravel a dark conspiracy. Justice, a manipulative human official, has stirred hatred between humans and the magical community, using enslavement collars and control over the Black Sun—an elite group of soldiers loyal to the Shadow Throne.

Just as civil war seems inevitable, Cal's Fate string—a magical bond tying him to his soulmate—leads him to a grim prison where he finds Haru, his bonded, broken and tortured. But Fate has more in store. Cal discovers he is bound not to one, but two: Rashi, a fox shifter, and Haru, a fierce dragon warrior. Together, this reluctant triad must face cult attacks, dark rituals, and the creeping Wound, a void threatening to consume their realm.

Cal's new reality is one of impossible choices—between duty and heart, loyalty and passion. As war looms, the only hope lies in Cal's ability to trust in his newfound soulmates and uncover the depths of the corruption before it's too late.

Scan the QR code below to order

www.ingramcontent.com/pod-product-compliance
Lightning Source LLC
LaVergne TN
LVHW050642100826
845148LV00011B/1947

* 9 7 8 1 6 4 1 0 8 8 9 1 6 *